The Eleventh Commandment

by

C. J. Carr

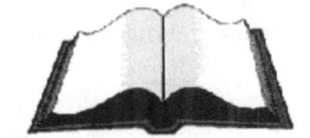

CCB Publishing
British Columbia, Canada

The Eleventh Commandment

Copyright ©2008 by C. J. Carr
ISBN-13   978-0-9810246-6-0
First Edition

Library and Archives Canada Cataloguing in Publication

Carr, C. J., 1935-
The Eleventh Commandment / written by C. J. Carr.
ISBN 978-0-9810246-6-0
I. Title.
PS3603.A7678E44 2008   813'.6   C2008-904919-5

Disclaimer: Although the story takes place in New York and Connecticut, the places and all people are purely the imagination of the author.

Extreme care has been taken to ensure that all information presented in this book is accurate and up to date at the time of publishing. Neither the author nor the publisher can be held responsible for any errors or omissions. Additionally, neither is any liability assumed for damages resulting from the use of the information contained herein.

Publisher: CCB Publishing
British Columbia, Canada
www.ccbpublishing.com

Dedication

A special thank you to
Gina Marie Di Donato
and
Leanne Franchville
For their original artwork on the cover

What are little girls made of, sugar and spice and everything deadly when you cross them.

PART ONE

CHAPTER ONE

THE BEGINNING

The teeming rain made it almost impossible for Frankie to drive. It took all her strength to keep the car from careening off the muddy, debris-ridden road. The local news had warned residents that, although the hurricane was moving out to sea, gale force winds were still expected and except for extreme emergencies all cars should stay off the road.

Frankie's side started to bleed again. She could feel the warm blood oozing out of the wound and soaking her shirt. Every time the old Chevy hit a rut in the road, the pain increased. Frankie winced as she leaned forward in the seat for a clearer view of the road through the straining windshield wipers. The high winds rocked the car like a cradle. Frankie gasped as a huge branch smashed into the windshield and shattered it. She closed her eyes against the spray of glass and slammed the brakes. She had been doing seventy miles per hour and was unable to control the car any longer. The Chevy skidded onto the auxiliary road and Frankie slammed the brakes again. This time, the car's right front and rear wheels lifted off the ground. As the car spun out of control it flipped over onto the roof knocking her unconscious.

Frankie woke to the smell of leaking gas. She was unaware of how long she had been unconscious, strapped in the seat of the wrecked car hanging upside down. Panicking, she loosened the seat belt and shifted her body around in the seat. Lifting both legs, she kicked the driver's side window out and crawled out onto the muddy road. Drenched, bleeding and breathing hard, Frankie crossed the road and squatted at its edge.

While the car was still running she could see smoke pouring from the engine. Seconds later, a fire ignited under the hood.

"Shit!" Frankie realized she had not grabbed her shoulder bag. She covered the wound in her side with one hand and ran back across the road to the car. She stretched her arm through the broken window and frantically fished around on the roof of the car for the leather bag, wallet, and most importantly, the gun, she would soon need. She pulled out the bag with the wallet still inside. But the gun was missing. She felt around for it along the roof and breathed a sigh of relief when her hand connected with the cool metal. She pulled it out and shoved it into the bag.

Frankie knew she had only seconds to run back to safety before the flames grew higher. She scrambled back across the road and into the thicket of woods, making it to safety just as the car exploded behind her. The force of the explosion lifted her off her feet and she dove head first into a pile of scrubby undergrowth. She lay there for a minute, covering her head with her arms while pieces of the exploded car rained down in the woods around her. Breathing hard, Frankie sat up and then knelt hunched over on the ground with her chin tucked into her chest, willing the strength to go on.

Her hatred for Doc was the only thing that kept her going. She grabbed onto the side of a nearby tree and slowly pulled herself to her feet, surveying her surroundings and the remains of the smoldering car across the road. She knew the road led to Doc's house. The thought of the bastard urged her on, and she picked her way through the fallen branches and debris from the car and back out to the road. Frankie walked for what seemed like hours in the lashing rain and wind, stumbling over branches and slogging through mud holes. The soles of her waterlogged shoes were coming un-glued when she finally

2

reached Doc's front gate. Exhausted and wild-looking, with her dark hair soaked and matted to her head and her wet clothes plastered to her thin and shivering body, Frankie shuffled along the graveled circular driveway to the front porch.

Frankie gripped the railing and painfully mounted the four steps. A bolt of lightning illuminated the porch and the old, weather beaten front door for a few seconds before the clap of thunder echoed above. Frankie reached into her shoulder bag and felt the smooth handle of the .38 inside. She moved closer to the front door and pushed the bell long and hard with her index finger. A few seconds passed and she pushed the bell again impatiently. "Come on!" she screamed inwardly. "Where is he?"

Behind the door, she heard Doc's heavy footsteps clunking along the wood floor of the hallway, and then his graveled voice. "Okay, okay. Hold on, I'm coming."

The porch light snapped on, startling Frankie for a moment. His face reddened when he saw her. Before he could shut the door, Frankie pulled the .38mm from her bag and shoved it into his throat. "Back up. Now stop and close your eyes and turn around slowly."

Doc held up both hands and backed up into the hallway. "Come on, Frankie. This isn't necessary."

She dug the gun deeper into his throat. "Shut your mouth and do what you're told. Move and I'll blow your head off."

He turned around and started to say something, but Frankie whipped him across the back of the head with the gun's barrel. Screaming from the searing pain he fell to his knees and put his hands up protectively around his head. "I said be quiet!" Frankie screamed over him. "Now get up and move slowly into the kitchen. I have a very nervous finger."

Still holding the back of his head, Doc managed to stand and stumbled down the hallway to the kitchen.

"Damn you, Frankie. You didn't have to do that."

"Shut up and sit down," she ordered, pointing to a chair at the table. She moved to the other side of the table and leaned against the countertop. She touched the bloodstained rip in her blouse. The pain in her side was almost unbearable now.

"You're bleeding. Let me help you," Doc said, trying to sound sincere as he started to rise from the chair.

"I said sit down!" Frankie fired the .38, and the bullet ripped through the edge of the table. Formica chips and wood splinters shot across the room. Doc covered his eyes with his hands.

"You're crazy, you know that? You could have blinded me!"

Frankie tried to stand up straight, but the pain in her side was getting to her. She was getting weaker and didn't know how much longer she could last. But she was going to kill Doc or die trying. She leaned back against the countertop, holding the gun in front of her with both hands.

"That's not all that's going to happen to you!" she screamed at him. "You killed Jason then tried to have *me* killed, you bastard! How could you do that? We loved you like a father. Damn you, Doc. To think I wished my own father was more like you. All I wanted was my cut. That's all any of us wanted. We trusted you, Doc. A lot of people are dead because of your greed."

Doc opened his mouth to protest, but Frankie pointed the .38 at him. "Doc, I can't think of a reason why I shouldn't kill you now."

"Look, I made a mistake. I swear your brother was becoming a liability, always demanding more and more money, so I had to do it."

"What about the others? Did you have to kill them, too?"

"Look, let's make a deal, okay? You come with me to

Europe and we'll split fifty, fifty. What do you say?" Doc
pleaded.

"You think that's going to make up for my brother?"

"I don't have to do anything if you want to be such a hard-
ass," he countered. You kill me and you get nothing. What do
you think of that?"

Frankie's side was throbbing and she felt light headed. She
knew she could pass out at any minute from the loss of blood.
Pain shot through her body again. Frankie dropped her guard
for a moment and Doc lunged over the table at her. The bullet
from her gun ripped through his chest, forcing his body
backwards over the chair. Doc slid down the blood soaked wall
and slumped over onto the floor.

Frankie walked around the table and stood at Doc's feet.
"That was a dumb move. You forgot commandment number
eleven --- never try to screw Frankie out of money. "

Doc looked up at her. Blood dripped from the side of his
lip. "You lose, baby," he said, managing a smile. "You'll never
find out where the jewels are hidden now."

"No, you lose, old man, because no matter how smart you
think you are, you have always been a creature of habit. I
already know where the diamonds are."

Frankie hit him across the face with the barrel of the .38,
and Doc slumped over on the floor. *I don't have to be afraid of
you anymore.* Picking up her shoulder bag, she shoved the .38
back into it. She walked back down the hallway, and leaning
on the railing, made it one step at a time up to the second floor
bedroom. Frankie had lost a great deal of blood, her body
ached with every step she took.

* * * * *

Sitting on the edge of the unmade bed, Frankie felt her

strength waning and nearly fainted. She managed to peel off her muddy clothes and inspected the wound. The bullet had sliced through her side, leaving a large gash. She felt unsteady as she reached for the bottle of bourbon on the dresser and took a swig. She knew she needed stitches. Frankie opened up the drawers in Doc's dresser, searching for a sewing kit. One thing about Doc, he was fastidious. He might be a thief, a liar and a murderer, but he always had his shirt buttons sewed on. In the third drawer, she found a small sewing kit. Frankie took another long pull from the bottle. Threading the needle with her unsteady hands took a little time. She laid the threaded needle on the bed and took two more long pulls from the bottle.

She looked around at the sparsely furnished room and caught a glimpse of herself in the dresser mirror. She held up the needle and thread. *"All I have is red thread,"* she said to a face she barely recognized. The sensation of passing out overcame her and her mud-caked face began to blur. *"Don't worry, Frankie. It's a nice color for stitches."* She took another pull from the bottle and started to sew. *"It doesn't hurt a bit, because my dear Francine, you're drunk,"* she said laughing to herself. She took what was left in the bottle and poured it over the wound, letting out a yell from the sting. *"Damn, that hurt. What a waste of good booze,"* she said, laughing again. Frankie stood on shaky legs and walked into the bathroom. She turned on the water, stepped into the shower and leaned back against the tiled wall, moving her head around to feel the full force of the hot spray. The rhythmic sound of the water mesmerized her as the scalding water penetrated her skin, turning it red. She closed her eyes, feeling a cloud of darkness engulf her. Frankie knew she had to lie down or she'd pass out right here in the shower and drown. *Which would be worse,* she thought, *bleeding to death or drowning? Silly me, you can't drown in a shower.*

Frankie got out of shower, and not bothering to dry off, went back to the bedroom and lay down on the bed. She glanced at the clock on the bedside table. It was 3 a.m. Frankie curled a pillow under her head and lay there exhausted, listening to the rain savagely beating against the widow. Doc was downstairs dead in the kitchen, and there was the strong possibility that she would bleed to death in the night. Frankie closed her eyes. She was beyond caring.

CHAPTER TWO

THE LONG RIDE HOME

Frankie awoke with a start, unsure at first of where she was. Faint sunlight streamed in through the white cotton curtains across the room. The rain had stopped, but the wind had not yet died down. She could still hear it howling around the house. She put a hand to the wound on her side and winced. Dried blood was caked around the opening. The stitches had held through the night, but she would have to get it treated by a doctor soon or risk getting an infection.

She rested against the pillows with one arm thrown up behind her head. Like a bad movie, her mind replayed the scenes of everything that had happened to her.

* * * * *

Frankie's thoughts drifted to the past. She had served six years of a ten-year prison term, thanks to Doc. She hadn't seen her family in all those years. She told herself the only reason she was going back to a mother, father and sister who hated her was just to get her clothes, but in her heart she knew differently. While she sat in prison, she thought only of seeing Doc and getting her share of the money. She'd have all the cash she would ever need, and that was all that mattered. Prison hadn't been so bad. It could have been worse. Some inmates had sucked up to her, really believing she had the money from the robbery stashed away. Her time in prison was in the past now.

There were only two things left to do now --- get her

money and find out who killed her brother. She thought that with Doc's help, finding her brother's killer would be easy. Frankie had loved Doc like a father. He had always been there for her, unlike her parents. But Doc could be ruthless and it scared her, now she realized just how ruthless he had been.

She would go back to New York and get the money. As soon as her business was finished, she would leave the city and start a new life for herself. It saddened her to know that there was no use trying to reconcile with her parents. She knew that was a waste of time, but she would try again.

* * * * *

Frankie sat up in bed and looked around the room. She needed a change of clothes as her jeans and shirt were in ruins from the mud and rain. She quickly decided to take something from Doc's closet to wear. She would then take the gun and drive Doc's car to the Greyhound station. However it was vital that she first cleared any evidence of having been in the house.

Normally, the long bus ride to New York would have been boring, but after six years in prison with nothing to look at but the concrete walls of her cell, Frankie thought she would find the scenery refreshing. Miles of highway would put a distance between the past and Doc lying dead in the kitchen. She now realized how much she'd taken her freedom for granted. The simple changing of the seasons, Fourth of July celebrations, a long walk were things she had never given a second thought to.

She had taken the rap for the robbery, never revealing the names of the others. Except for her brother, Jason, she never knew who they were, until a year later when Jason came to visit her and gave her the names. Doc told her that what she didn't know, she couldn't tell. She had to keep her brother out of jail because she knew Doc was right. Jason would crack under the pressure and they would all be up shit's creek without a paddle and Jason would be killed. Doc had him hidden away so the police couldn't find him.

They had threatened to kill Jason, but she didn't think Doc would be the one to do it in the end. She knew this situation was of her brother's own doing. She knew him for what he was: nothing more then a petty thief who usually wound up biting off more than he could chew and then crying like a baby when he got caught.   She had always protected him, her precious little brother, and most of the time took the blame for his misfortunes. Not that she felt she was any better; she loved living on the edge but was smart enough not to get caught.

Frankie knew it would break her parents' hearts if they knew the truth about Jason, the baby of the family, so she was content to remain the sole black sheep of the family.

After six years in a six-by-nine cell, Frankie was happy to finally be out and going somewhere. She mounted the steps onto the bus and looked around. Even the old Greyhound --- a source of freedom since it would carry her miles and miles away from here --- looked good to her. She walked up the aisle to an empty window seat in the back so she could enjoy the scenery on the way home. She had a great deal of time to think in prison, and it was the one place she didn't want to visit again.

The only information she could find while she was locked up, was that her brother had been shot dead in an alley in what the cops called "a drug deal gone wrong." That didn't sound right to her, unless things had changed, because Jason never messed with drugs and was deathly afraid of guns.

Frankie knew that her family would never believe her story about going straight. Her parents had heard it too many times, but this time it was the truth. The money would change her life.

Her father had visited her only once in the six years she was in prison, and blamed her for Jason's death. He said it was her bad influence that got him killed. That was the last time she saw either of them. She closed her eyes and leaned back against the vinyl seat, letting memories of her and Jason sitting at the back of the poolroom in Doc's office came to mind.

* * * * *

"We just pulled off one of the biggest heists in more than twenty years. There's more than sixty million dollars in uncut diamonds here. Do you realize what we accomplished? We did a job that even a pro would have backed away from and it came off like clockwork. You're going to blow it now?" Doc raged, pointing a finger at Jason. His red face was twisted in an angry snarl. He ran his hands through his thick gray hair in exasperation.

"We all agreed, once the job was finished we would hide the diamonds until the heat dies down. Then we'd sell them on the European market!" Doc paced the floor with his hands on his hips.

Jason sat quietly, his chin in his hands. Frankie glanced at his young, handsome face.

"Look, I wasn't in on this job, so what's it got to do with me?" Frankie interrupted. She stood up to leave.

"No, you stay," Doc ordered. "This has something to do with you."

"Yeah, Like how?"

"Your shit-head brother stole one of the diamonds and tried to hock it, even after I told everyone not to change their routine and stay out of trouble. We needed to wait six – only six --- months until we sold the uncut diamonds. We pulled off a professional job, and then your brother got greedy and screwed things up."

"Want me to slap his fingers?" She said sarcastically.

"No, Frankie, I want you to take the rap for him!"

"What, are you crazy? You got some pair of balls! You don't let me in on this job and now you want me to take the rap, no way." Frankie headed toward the door.

"If the cops get hold of this jerk, we'll all be in jail the same day," Doc warned.

"I'm sorry, but there isn't anything you can say to change my mind. The answer is no. I'm tired of taking the rap for him!"

"Frankie, I'd kill him first before I'd go to prison."

Frankie laughed. "Be my guest."

"One-third of sixty million dollars sound good."

"You said the magic word. But I have a better deal in mind --- one-third plus one million for every year I serve. After all, it's me that's going to sit in prison."

"It's a deal." Doc said.

Frankie relaxed and let herself drift off into sleep. It would be at least 20 hours before she got to New York. The ribbon of highway stretching between Florida and the Big Apple was a long one.

*   *   *   *   *

Frankie stood in front of the old three-story brownstone. They had lived on the first two floors and rented the third to a schoolteacher. She remembered something her mother had told her before she'd left for prison. *Frankie, people come and go, but the Bronx always stays the same and will never change because of people like you.* Frankie started to walk away, wanting to melt into the flow of people streaming down the sidewalk and just disappear. She could take the subway back to the Port Authority and hop another bus and get the hell out of here and never face her family again. But she stopped to take one last look at the building and thought *hell, Frankie you may as well go in and get it over with.*

Frankie mounted the eight steps to the front door and rang the bell of her parents' apartment. Behind the door she heard the muffled sound of slippered feet shuffling down the hallway. The door opened and her mother appeared. Sophia's face drained of color at the sight of her daughter.

"Francine! I, I thought you were still in prison!"

"Don't worry, I didn't escape. I got out early for good behavior. Can I come in and get my stuff?"

Still in shock, Sophia stood in silence for a moment, searching Frankie's face. This was not the Francine she remembered. Her brown eyes had always been soft and loving when she was a child, now they looked hard and callous, and it saddened her.

"Wait here a minute. I'll be right back."

Still standing on the stairs, Frankie leaned against the door to keep it open. She could hear her father's rumbling voice coming from somewhere within the depths of the apartment. The sounds were muffled, but she knew she would not be welcome. On his one and only visit to her in prison, he had told her that she no longer existed; that she was dead to him for what she did to her brother. She would never forget the dead look in his eyes as he looked at her through the panel of clear plastic that separated them in the visiting room "Daddy! No! You don't understand! Please!" She had cried like a frightened child. But Aaron had already risen from his chair and was asking the officer to let him out.

Frankie brushed the memory from her mind. She knew she was not wanted here and started to turn around and head back down the steps when her mother re-appeared.

"Come in," Sophia said, smoothing the skirt of her flowered housedress, an unconscious grooming action she had. Frankie followed her mother in through the narrow kitchen past her father, who was sitting at the table reading the newspaper and doing his best to ignore his daughter's presence. Sophia led her down the hallway and up the flight of stairs to the bedrooms above. Frankie's mother opened the door to her daughter's childhood bedroom and stepped back to let her in. All of her things --- school photos, knickknacks, stuffed animals, and other treasures Frankie had collected as a girl - had been packed up. The room was bare except for the furniture.

"Your father said to take what's yours and leave. I asked him to let you stay, but you know how stubborn he is. In time he will get over it," her mother said sadly.

"Yes mom. I know how stubborn the European mind can be. Maybe he will forget --- when hell freezes over," she replied sarcastically, reaching to open the top draw of her dresser.

"Where will you go, Frankie?" her mother asked tearfully. She was sitting on the edge of the bed watching her daughter.

"Why the hell do you care? For that matter, why do any of you care?"

"Don't say that, Frankie. I *do* care. Your father cares, but he still mourns the loss of Jason. Six years is a long time for self-pity."

"Or is it just that hating me is an easy way to keep from blaming himself?" Frankie said bitterly.

"You should not talk about your father that way."

"Maybe it was my fault. If I hadn't taken the rap for him, Jason would still be alive. Then my father would only hate me for his precious son being in jail. Cruel world, isn't it, mom?" Frankie snapped back.

"Please, Frankie! Stop talking like that!"

Frankie finished stuffing all of her belongings into an old duffel bag she found in the closet. "I'm packed. You want to check and see if I stole anything?"

"Frankie why do you always antagonize the people who love you?"

"People who love me, Okay, let's count them, Mama." Her mother stood silently before her with tears running down her cheeks. A piece of her beautiful dark hair, tucked up in a neat bun, had fallen out of place and caressed her right cheek. As a child, Frankie had always loved her mother's hair and would happily spend hours brushing it and playing with it while she and Sophia talked about everything from dolls to boys.

"Now that they're all counted," Frankie snarled, "let me tell you something, my dear mother. *I* took the rap for your wonderful son. And you know it, because he told you so. And you never said anything to Dad, not a thing. You let him keep thinking that it was my fault."

Frankie threw the duffel bag over her shoulder. "I got one last thing to say to you. Your golden boy was a thief. He was born one and he died one. And there was nothing you or my dear, dear father could have ever done about it. And as far as my slut sister is concerned, well, you can all kiss my ass. That is about as much respect as all of you will get from me."

* * * * *

Sophia knew in her heart that some of what Frankie had said was true. She had been taught from childhood that a woman's place was in the kitchen. When Aaron told her that, he feared that war in Europe was a great possibility, and they would be able to have and raise a family in this land of opportunity.

Sophia thought that coming to America would have changed things, but it didn't. They just resumed the old ways. She knew Francine was right --- she and Aaron were living in the past, while their children grew up in the present. What bothered her most was realizing that if she and Aaron did not change, Francine would be lost to them forever.

* * * * *

Frankie stood in front of Snookies poolroom, looking around at the familiar surroundings. *Some things never change, do they?* She lifted the duffel bag over her shoulder and walked in, hearing familiar voices calling out. As she walked towards the back of the room, she saw Theo guarding the office door. Theo had been Doc's bodyguard since she was a kid. "Yo, Theo. How's it going?"

Theo's six-foot-seven body filled the door frame. He looked down at Francine with approval in his steel brown eyes. "Well, little lady, I see they let you out early."

"I want to see Doc."

"Wait here, little lady"

"It's only me, Theo." Frankie said.

"You know the rules. You haven't been away that long little lady."

Frankie dropped the duffel bag in front of her and waited as Theo went into the office closing the door behind him.

Theo stepped out of the office a few seconds later. "Okay. Leave the bag here and go in."

"Still don't trust anyone, huh?" Frankie smiled teasingly and walked past him into the office.

"That's my job," Theo said with pride.

Doc stood up as she came in. "Frankie, glad to see you out early, you do know why I couldn't come to see you."

Frankie nodded, acknowledging she knew the reason, and sat in the chair in front of the desk. *The same old place it hasn't changed in six years, and I guess it never will, either.*

"Let me get you a beer." Doc walked over to the refrigerator, opening the door and took out two bottles. Handing one to Frankie, he added, "I'll bet you missed one of these in the slammer" he remarked as he sat down.

Frankie twisted the cap off, taking a long swig, and then she smiled. "You're right; I sure did miss a nice ice cold beer."

"What can I do for you now that you're home again?" Doc asked cheerfully.

"Do for me? Well, you can give me my money. Then you can tell me who killed my brother."

"One thing I always liked about you Frankie, you don't waste words. But there is no money, not just yet."

"What the hell are you talking about? You said you would wait a few months and sell the diamonds on the European market, and when I got out the money would be waiting for me. What the hell are you trying to pull!

"Calm down I know what I said. But nobody's got anything yet."

Frankie stood up saying "now--."

Doc interrupted her, "Wait a second, please, sit down, and don't get excited till I explain. I made a contact through a friend in Amsterdam and by waiting till the statute of limitations ran out I could get the diamonds cut, we would all come away with almost eight to ten million more by waiting the full seven years." Doc said, almost out of breath.

"I don't like this, you better be on the level, Doc."

"My God, Frankie, why would I lie about a thing like that, there are too many people involved in this, all of whom could put me a way for a long time. Frankie, I'm surprised at you. Haven't I always treated you and your brother like you were my own kid?"

"I'm sorry Doc" Frankie said, smiling, "I remember when you used to help me with my homework after we pulled a scam," she reminisced.

"Your used gum is still stuck under the edge of the desk. Yeah, those were the good days, things have gotten too complicated," he said, reminiscing.

Frankie stood up and walked to the refrigerator for another beer. "Well Doc, you taught me never to trust anyone,"

"I didn't mean me," Doc said in a joking manner.

"Tell me about my brother, Doc, because I find all this hard to believe, He never did drugs, and was deathly afraid of guns, so this situation doesn't feel right to me."

"You don't have to be on drugs to sell them. I warned him against it. But you know Jason. He always had to do things his way, and as usual he bit off more then he could chew. He figured he could make more money selling drugs than working with me."

Doc continued talking as he opened the top drawer of his desk.

"You know I never got mixed up with that stuff, so I don't have any connections in this area. You know there is very little that goes on that I don't know, but this time everyone clammed up, maybe you'll have better luck but I doubt it," he said, sounding sincere.

Frankie sat listening. "I have to try and find out what happened, Doc."

"I know. When we finalize the deal you get both your share and your brother's. Maybe your family could use the money. Meanwhile, here is fifteen hundred to get you started. I have a few small jobs going, you want in?"

Frankie stood up put her arm around Doc. "Thanks for your help and your offer, but I think I am going to play it safe for now."

"A word of advice... your brother was in with some scary people, so be careful. Be patient, the year is almost over and you'll get your money; forget this obsession about finding your brother's killer. It can only get you hurt."

"Thanks for the help and the word, Doc; I'll keep in touch."

Opening the door to leave, she looked at Doc once more. Frankie started to say something, but decided not to. Walking out of Doc's office she picked up her duffel bag. "See you around, Theo."

"Take care, little lady," Theo said in his bass voice.

Standing outside the poolroom, she thought for a moment and came to the conclusion that although Doc sounded truthful, she didn't know why, but she felt there was something wrong with his story. Still, she just couldn't put her finger on it. Frankie was confused at this point. Doc had always treated her and Jason well; he was more like a father than her own father.

"This matter was too much for her to think about on her first day out of prison. *What I need is a place to stay and some rest. I'll figure everything out later.* Walking to the corner payphone, she dropped the duffel bag and looked through her purse for some change. Putting the coins in, she dialed. The phone rang, and she heard the same old voice on the other end. "Your dime your time. One Hour Cleaner's, Midge speaking."

"It's me, Frankie, can you pick me up? I'll be in front of Snookies."

"Son of a bitch, you didn't break out, did you, Frankie."

Frankie started to laugh. "Don't get excited! I'm out early, and I need a place to crash for a while."

The voice on the other end sounded excited. "No problem, you can have your old room back, be there to get you in a jiff." The phone line went dead.

Frankie knew if there was one person in the world she could depend on it was Midge. Unlike her parents, who had walked away from her, Midge had been there for her more times than she could remember. She knew that if it hadn't been for Doc and Midge she didn't know what would have happened to her.

19

* * * * *

Midge had always been a flirt and had known Frankie since grade school. The boys were a bit cautious when it came to Frankie, especially after she hit Jackie Ross in the head with a baseball bat for feeling her ass. She had come to Midge's aid more than once though. Midge's flirtation had got her into trouble with the boys on many occasions; one time, three boys had dragged her into the boys' bathroom after school in an attempt to rape her. If Frankie had not been there looking for her at that time, there's no telling what could have happened to Midge. Frankie had always looked out for her, and there wasn't anything Midge would not do for her. Although they were the same age Midge had taken a different path in life. She had met Otto and even though he was ten years her senior she had fallen madly in love with him. Despite the objections of her family they married the day after her graduation. Seeing Frankie on the corner, she made an illegal u-turn on the avenue. Slamming the brakes as she reached the curb, Midge slid across the seat of the van. She yelled out Frankie's name and before her feet hit the ground the two women were embracing each other.

* * * * *

Frankie looked around the apartment. The sink was piled up with dishes, clothes thrown everywhere. "I see this place hasn't changed much," Frankie said, smiling.

"Oh, but yes, they have," Midge, said walking over to the refrigerator. "Do you want a beer?"

"Yes that sounds good. What do you mean, things have changed? Everything looks the same to me," Frankie said, laughing.

"I finally dumped Eddie. Don't you notice his junk is

missing?"

"Who could tell what's missing under all this. But I am glad you wised up." Midge put her hands at her side, pretending her feelings were hurt. "You know, Frankie, you came out of prison a snob."

"Who, me, a snob?"

"Yes, you," Midge said, emptying the contents of Frankie's duffel bag on the floor. "There now, things look real neat now."

"Midge, you're still a nut," Frankie laughed. The women embraced again.

"I'm glad you're back, Frankie. Look, why don't you get some rest and we'll clean up this mess later, then we can talk."

"Yea, I am exhausted," Frankie said, sitting on the bed.

"I got to get back to the cleaners before my two losers rob me blind. Get some rest…chow, baby." Midge said leaving.

Frankie lay down and closed her eyes; she could remember the last time she met with Doc before she went to jail. "Look kid" Doc had said. "You're not eighteen yet, you're still a minor, and the worst that could happen is you get six years with good behavior. You'll be 23 when you get out, figure it as a paid vacation.'

"Some vacation," Frankie remarked

"All Jason has to say is he stole it from you and tried to hock it. Your money will be here waiting for you when you get out."

She remembered saying to Doc "As long you don't forget Frankie's eleventh commandment; if you do there will be hell to pay."

Frankie remembered going through hours of interrogation. She had been offered immunity if she talked, and. her refusal was frustrating to the interrogators. There were some who suspected the truth, but it could never be proven. Frankie was tried as a juvenile since she was not yet eighteen at the time.

* * * * *

Frankie awoke to the smell of fresh brewed coffee. Sitting at the edge of the bed she yawned. Standing, she walked lazily across the hall to the kitchen. Midge was sitting at the table in her nightshirt with a mug in her hand.

"Hey, sleepyhead, you're finely up."

"What time is it?" Frankie asked, opening the cabinet door to look for a cup.

"Time?" Midge asked. "You mean, what day is it?"

Frankie sat down and poured herself a cup of coffee. "You should have awakened me sooner," she finally said, sipping her coffee.

"You looked so peaceful I didn't have the heart. Relax and have a quiet day. By the way, you can have a job at the cleaners if you want it."

"Thanks, Midge, you seem to be the only one I can depend on."

"No thanks necessary, you've done a lot for me," Midge said

I have a ten o'clock appointment with my parole officer tomorrow, and I got some things to take care of."

"What's his name; maybe I know him." Midge said, winking her eye.

"Harry Wise," Frankie answered.

"Yeah, I know him. He's a real sleaze bag. If he gives you a problem, call Doc. He can fix things for you," Midge replied.

"Look, tomorrow is Friday, go see Wise then relax for the day. You can start work on Monday, how's that?" Midge said, leaving the kitchen.

"That's good. By the time I clean this place up it will

probably be Monday," Frankie teased. Then she spent an hour hanging up her clothes and cleaning the room she'd slept in. Going through her stuff, she had picked a dress that she felt was conservative enough to wear to the parole office. Measuring it against her body, she thought, *this one will do... not too long... short knee length should do it...and, now, for a non-revealing top.*

* * * * *

Frankie hung her ironed clothes on the bathroom door-hook. She stripped down. Looking into the mirror she posed, checking her ribs. She had lost weight in prison.   A few adjustments the dress would be ok. *In a few weeks I'll get all the weight back.* Adjusting the water temperature, she stepped into the shower.

* * * * *

The interview with her parole officer had gone the way she had been told by her cellmates it would. She heard the rules and regulations, and the many threats he used trying to scare her. So he would check out her job and her apartment time from to time. *Big deal,* she thought.

Frankie had decided to stop at the cleaner's and have lunch with Midge. Traffic was heavy and it had taken longer than usual to reach her stop. After being away for so long the ride was still enjoyable. The bus stopped at One Hundred and Fifty-Fifth Street, where the cleaner was located. Midge had inherited the business from her late husband, Otto. Business had always been good, but Otto was always looking to make an easy buck, so he had worked out a deal with some people to use his place as a local drop for the numbers racket. Unfortunately, Otto had a sticky finger and his employers didn't like it.

Walking towards the store she saw Tony D, who looked up as he came out of the cleaners. "Frankie, I heard you were out," he said, grabbing her hands and gently pushing her away from him. "Let me see... prison didn't do you any harm. You still look good, baby."

Frankie smiled. She had known him since she was twelve years old. She gave him a kiss on the cheek, and then asked, "Where you headed?"

"Just finishing up my rounds... couple stops more to go. Hey, why don't you stop at the Irish pub tonight? We can talk over old times."

"Sounds good; see you tonight," Frankie said. Tony waved to her as he crossed the street. Frankie watched him as he disappeared into the crowd. Frankie walked into the store. Midge was on the phone and motioned to Frankie to wait a second. Looking around, she noticed that the place had finally been redecorated.

Midge hung up the phone as Frankie came behind the counter. "Well, how do you like the way the place looks?" Midge said with pride.

"The place looks great. It's about time you spent some of that money you have hidden under your mattress."

"They teach you to be a smart-ass in prison," Midge joked.

Frankie smiled. "I just met Tony D at the corner."

"Yeah, he just left here."

"I know. He invited me out for drinks. I'd feel better if you came with me." Midge frowned. "No, honey, you go and have a good time."

"Please come with me; I have to ask some questions and I would feel better if you were with me."

"I really don't want to.... okay."

* * * * *

Tony met them at the front door. "Frankie, Midge, come on, I have a table in the back. You two take beer, if I remember," he said. They moved slowly through the Friday night crowd to their table. Frankie had decided to wait until Tony had a little more to drink before she tried to get any information out of him. As usual, Midge was table-hopping, leaving Frankie to dance with Tony most of the evening. "How about dumping her and going to my place? I can help you make up for the time you've been away. You know what I mean, Baby-face," Tony added, forcing her closer to him. "We'll talk about it later. Who knows... you may get lucky if things turn out the way I like."

They were sitting at the table when Midge returned, saying, "I'm getting too old for this life. I've got to sit down."

The look on Tony's face showed that he might be ready to talk.

"Is that how I am going to feel when I hit forty?" Frankie asked playfully.

"Oh boy, you're going to get yours," Midge said as they laughed.

"In that case," Tony said, "which one of you is coming home with me tonight? Hell, the way I feel, I could take on the two of you."

"Tony," Frankie said seriously, "I need some information."

"Sure, a little sack time and I'll do my best to help you if I can."

"I want to know who killed my brother. And the real reason why."

Tony's expression changed. He seemed to have sobered up.

"You want to get into my pants. You have to give something in return," Frankie challenged.

"Look, Frankie, let it lay. Jay is dead and there is nothing anyone can do about it. From what I understand he was involved with some bad people. That's all I know about it." Tony responded, sounding a bit shaky.

"I don't believe you. Give me a name. One name," Frankie urged.

"Frankie, I swear I can't help you; I don't know."

Frankie stood up and slipped into the seat next to him. As she did, Frankie slammed the edge of her bottle against the table, breaking it, and then shoved the jagged ends between his legs. He winced. "You're crazy, Frankie. I swear I don't know anything." She pressed the jagged ends of the bottle in, almost ripping his pants. "Yes, I am crazy. Midge, have I ever gone back on a promise? "

"No, I don't think you have, come to think about it." Midge could see the pain in his face.

"Now," Frankie said, "just one name and no lies or I am going to cut your balls off." Tony was breathing hard now.

"Okay, okay, a guy called the Spaniard; he had dealings with Jay. He may know something; he works as a mule sometimes."

"Where do I find him?"

"I don't know. I swear."

Frankie applied a little more pressure, ripping the material on his pants. "I said where!"

"Yankee Stadium, he hawks tickets before the game as a sideline. Now please stop."

Frankie dropped the bottle as she stood. "Come on, let's go," she said to Midge.

"Hey, Tony, no hard feelings," Frankie said as they left.

"I guess he won't get laid tonight," Midge said, joking.

"No," Frankie said, "I think he shit his pants."

* * * * *

Frankie was quiet on the ride home. "Cat got your tongue?" Midge asked, breaking the silence.

"I was just thinking…. It was stupid to get you involved in all this."

"Why, because I am the one Tony picks up money from-- one of the mob's numbers drop? Don't worry about it. You think he's going to say some broad stuck a broken bottle up his crotch and he shit himself? Trust me, he's not."

"Just the same," Frankie replied. I'll see this thing out, myself, just in case something goes wrong."

Midge was silent for a few seconds, then she pulled the van over to the curb. "Listen, tough gal. I am already in this thing. Who are you staying with? Who gave you a job? Who is helping you get information? Me, that's who, so cut out this loner crap. I am in this thing right up to my neck. So, don't get noble on me now."

"Midge you don't owe me anything. What I did for you, I did because of our friendship," Frankie replied.

Midge turned to Frankie, saying, "I said I'm in this thing with you, and that's it!" Frankie was silent for a second, and knowing there was nothing she could say to

Change Midge's mind, she finally said, "Okay, but remember if things get too complicated, you're out of this for good."

"All right, it's a deal. Now let's get some sleep," Midge said yawning.

"I'm going to need a gun," Frankie said.

"Do you thing that's a good idea?" Midge answered, very concerned.

"Yes I do. You know some people, so set me up with someone, okay?"

"Well, my dear, you're in luck. Our old friend Johnny Brown is back in town."

Frankie laughed, saying. "You're kidding! I thought he retired after his last con went bad."

"No, he's back in business again. He is now the Reverend Johnson Brown of the Church of Lost Souls, in Queens. If anyone can get you a gun, it's him."

"I'll stop in and see him tomorrow. It will be good to see Johnny again after all these years," Frankie said. She remembered working with him off and on for almost a year when she had been eleven. Frankie sighed to herself, realizing that she had been a thief almost her entire life; even then, living on the edge gave her a rush

* * * * *

Frankie arrived at the Church of Lost Souls just as Pastor Johnson Brown was saying to his last church member, "Good day, brother Archer, I hope you enjoyed the services." Then, turning, he saw Frankie. "Well, Sister Rose, welcome back to the flock. You have been sorely missed," he preached, as he hugged her.

"I need a favor Johnny," she whispered in his ear.

"Follow me. What can I do for you to help you find salvation?" They entered the church walking to the back of the building. "In here," he said, pointing to the door on the right marked 'Pastor's Office.' Frankie looked around the freshly painted office, then smiled, saying, "Johnny Brown, you old fraud; still packing them in I see. How is Lilly?"

"I miss the old girl, but she will be out next month."

"I need a gun, Johnny."

"Graduating to the big time, I see."

"How about a drink first?" he said, pulling a bottle of scotch and two glasses out of his desk drawer.

"You sure that's what you want; you never needed one before," Johnny asked, puzzled.

"Jason is dead and I want his killer dead," Frankie replied in anger.

"I heard about what happened, but as a friend, I have to tell you that the gun won't solve anything," Johnny said with concern.

"I don't need a lecture, just a gun!" Frankie insisted.

"All right, but one word of caution. In my business I hear things that most of the big boys don't. No one is talking about this, some say he was working for a mystery man. My advice is watch out for the people close to you," Johnny warned.

"You know something you're not telling me?" Frankie asked.

"No more than I have told you. Now, if you are still determined to have a gun, ask and you shall receive--for a price, of course," he added.

"I need some extra ammo."

"I think I have what you want." He walked over to a blackboard hanging on the wall. He lifted the six-by-three-foot board. Behind it were several dozen pistols and assault weapons. "I have an idea. Forget this madness and come and work with me and Lilly again for a while. It would be like old times. I have some new gimmicks. Remember the little girl act we use to pull off, how about it. You don't need a gun for that."

"Thank you anyway, Johnny. But, I've got to find a killer. How much you asking for the .38?"

He put his hand to his chin as though deep in thought. "A revelation has come to me. For you, Sister Frankie, five hundred, and I am not even breaking out even on this deal."

"I'll bet you're not; three hundred and you have a deal," Frankie said, smiling.

"O.K., that sounds good." Frankie stuck the .38 into her shoulder bag.

He worried that she would get in over her head with this quest of hers. He walked her to the front steps. "Be careful kid, remember what I said," he warned as Frankie walked away.

"You sure you won't change your mind?" he called out. He wished there was something he could do to help her. He just hoped that she got through this thing in one piece.

* * * * *

The Yankees were out of town and wouldn't be back until Monday, so Frankie decided to see if she could pick up some leads on her brother's killer. Frankie needed the van for her Saturday deliveries. She could use the van Sunday because the cleaner's was closed.

For some reason, she thought she was being followed. At first she thought she was just being paranoid. She tried switching trains twice, but the feeling lingered. Frankie couldn't think of any reason why anyone would want to follow her, unless Tony had sent someone to get even with her for embarrassing him at the club. She decided if she was being followed to give her shadow a tour of the city. *Stop imagining things. Go home and get some rest. Take a hot bath and get a good night's sleep. Tomorrow's another day.*

* * * * *

The *Daily News* sports page said the game started at 2:15, so she had plenty of time to get her work done and take the van up to the stadium. If the parole officer showed up, Midge could say that Frankie was out on her route. She had told Midge she thought someone had been following her, and was surprised by Midge's concern, because she took very little seriously.

* * * * *

It was almost 12:30 when Frankie finished loading the van. She knew not all of the stops were legitimate. Some were just Midge's pick-up places. Every Friday evening, Tony D picked up the money that had been bet on the numbers and delivered it to his boss. Winners were paid off on Saturday morning. They had a good system--the receipts and money were sown into certain garments

"Look, the route hasn't changed. You'll see the same old faces. Remember to finish your route before you do anything else. We don't want to get anyone mad at us."

"Don't worry. I'll take care of business first," Frankie assured Midge.

Out of the corner of her eye, Midge saw Jack Wise coming up the block. She nudged Frankie. "Your PO is here."

Frankie turned as he walked into the shop. He reached out and put a hand on her shoulder. She shrugged it off. "I ain't your leaning post."

"You should be a little nicer to me, I could do a lot for a babe like you," he said, red-faced. "Or, I could fix it for you to go back and finish out your time. Know what I mean?"

Midge knew Jack had been on the take, with an envelope a week when he was on the force, and as far as she knew, he still got a little taste of the action.

"Listen, you fat sleaze bag. You want to send me back? Go ahead. But let me give you a little present before you send me back." And pulled out a bat from under the counter where Midge kept it for emergencies.

Jack tried to wrestle the bat out of her hands, but Frankie stepped back out of his reach and held it up threateningly. "Look, pal, keep your damned hands to yourself. You want to send me back? For what? Because I hurt your ego?" Frankie shouted.

Midge moved between them. "Hey, Jack. It's her first work day. There's a lot of pressure on her. Come on. Cut her some slack," Midge said.

"Nobody talks to me like that, especially no two-bit con."

"Look, Jack. The fact is my friend is high-strung. She gets upset easy. Now, how about you being a good guy," Midge pleaded.

Jack hesitated, and then backed up a few steps. "Okay, Midge. For you, just this one time."

"Thanks Jack."

He pointed at Frankie. "I'll see you again, only next time it will be different." Jack strode over to the door, jerked it open and stormed out.

Frankie was breathing heavily and her eyes were full of rage.

"What the hell? Are you crazy?" Midge screamed. "I told you a long time ago your temper is going to get you killed." She yanked the bat out of Frankie's hands and put it back under the counter.

"I'm sorry. I'll try to keep calm next time."

"Get hold of Doc. He owes you a few favors. He should be able to get this freak off your case."

Frankie was silent for a few seconds. "You think he can take care of this matter?"

"I know so," Midge said confidently.

"You better get going or you're going to be late. And please don't screw up the van. Be careful."

They walked out of the shop where the van was parked on the curb.

Frankie climbed into the driver's seat, put the key in the ignition and revved up the engine just to upset Midge. She gave Midge a quick smile and peeled off.

On game days, traffic was always heavy. Still, Frankie managed to get to the stadium twenty minutes early. She drove slowly through the hoards of game-goers gathered at each entrance of the huge stadium. She got lucky. On the second pass, she spotted him. He was of medium height, and wore a skintight tee-shirt and equally tight jeans. A blue bandana was wrapped around his dark hair.

Frankie was lucky again and found a parking spot not too far away. She hopped into the back of the van and started pawing through the racks of clothes. *This should do.* She held up a miniskirt and a low-cut red blouse. The name on the tag said Jennifer Lewis. Frankie didn't think she would mind. Besides, it was for a good cause.

Frankie stripped off her work clothes and made a hasty change. *If this doesn't get him, nothing will.* She jumped out of the back of the van, slammed the doors shut and took off across the parking lot, putting a little extra swing into her walk. He was easy to spot in the crowd with the blue bandana, and she walked in his direction. He noticed her and smiled broadly.

"Hey, babe. What you doing?" he said in a heavy Puerto Rican accent.

"Not much, amigo. How about a ticket to the game?"

"Only got two left. You don't look like you got much to bargain with."

"How about we take it out in trade, Amigo," Frankie said suggestively, rubbing her breasts.

"Hell, momma. You think you can take what I got?"

"Come on over to my van and let's see what you got, stud."

He hesitated and Frankie realized she was losing him. "Why am I wasting my time with a loser like you anyway?" she said with a laugh, and started to walk away.

"What the hell you laughing at, bitch?"

"Faggot." Frankie said giving him the finger.

"Yeah, bitch. Come on. I'm going to give you something to put you in heaven. You're gonna call me Daddy after I'm finished with you."

He followed her to the van and opened the back doors. He hopped up and reached out a hand to her.

"Welcome to my home," she said, clambering in, slamming the doors behind her. "Let's go, stud. Show me what you got."

He laughed. "Okay, baby. Get ready for heaven."

He pulled off his sneakers and started to undo the buckle on his belt. "I hope you can take what I got, baby."

It's now or never, she thought. Frankie reached into her tote bag, pulled out the .38 and pointed it at him.

"You bitch!" he yelled, standing there with his pants pooled around his ankles. "You ain't gonna get away with this. I'm gonna find you and cut your heart out!"

"Shut up," Frankie said calmly.

He pulled a switchblade out of a sock.

Frankie cocked the .38 and said, "Don't be stupid. You'll be dead before you can throw it."

He hesitated, took a deep breath and dropped the knife.

"I don't want your stinking money. Just answer some questions and you can leave here alive. Who killed my brother Jay?"

"That faggot was your brother?" he asked sarcastically. Frankie pulled the trigger and the lead slug whistled between his legs, ripping through the front seat. He clamped his hands over his ears. "You're crazy. You want to kill me?"

"I will, if you don't tell me what I want to know."

He dropped to his knees.

"Here, take the money. There's six hundred bucks here." He reached under the band of his other sock and pulled out a wad of cash.

Frankie cocked the .38 again. "This time I won't miss."

The Spaniard was breathing heavily. He begged her to take the money and leave.

"Goodbye, Amigo."

"No, wait! I'll tell you what you want to know."

Frankie smiled saying, "Good. Now we are getting somewhere. So, who killed my brother?"

"Damn, I should have known who you were. You're the crazy bitch that almost cut off Tony D's balls!"

Frankie laughed. "You're next."

"I swear, man. I don't know. I don't know anything!"

Frankie cocked the hammer again.

"Wait, wait. I met your brother the night he was killed. He was my weekly contact; we usually met at Kelly's. We took care of business and usually had a few drinks. But he was in a hurry that night; said he had to meet with someone else. That's all I know, I swear it."

"Who was he working for?"

"I don't know; nobody knows. All I know is he did jobs for Doc Murdock. That's it, I swear."

Frankie backed out of the van again, leaving both doors open. "Beat it."

The Spaniard backed slowly out of the van and dropped down onto the pavement. He turned to walk away, but when he was at a safe distance he turned around. "Nobody makes a fool out of the Spaniard and lives long enough to enjoy it. You're dead, bitch." He drifted off into the crowd, and eventually Frankie lost sight of him.

Frankie was more confused now than she had been in the beginning. It couldn't be Doc; he never dealt in drugs before, so why would he start now, especially with all those diamonds at risk? *I have to sort this thing out. I will have to talk to Doc again.*

Frankie changed back into her work clothes and hung

Jennifer Lewis's outfit back in their plastic coverings. She hadn't worn them very long. Jennifer would never know. Frankie got behind the wheel, ready to continue her route. *Midge is going to have a fit about her front seat.*

* * * * *

Frankie pulled up in front of the cleaners and went around opening the back doors. She pulled out the basket with the clothes she had collected on her route and rolled it into the shop. Midge always left the door open in the summer months so she didn't have to run the air-conditioner.

"How was your first day?" Midge asked cheerfully.

"Not bad. Here are the receipts for the day."

"No, I mean the meeting with the Spaniard."

"What a sleaze bag. I am more confused now than ever. I'll tell you about it on the way home."

At the end of the day, after the final chores had been completed, Midge's curiosity got the better of her.

"Look," she said. "Everyone is gone and we're closed and I can't wait. So, tell all."

Frankie told Midge everything that had transpired between her and the Spaniard, leaving out the fact that she had blown a hole in the front seat of the van.

"That's it? There's something you're not telling me. What is it?"

"That's it," Frankie lied.

"You forget one thing. I know you and I can tell when something is wrong."

"I blew a hole in the front seat of the van," Frankie said sheepishly.

Midge's mouth opened as she sank into her chair. "You what?" she asked incredulously.

"I shot a hole in the front seat of your van."

36

"You shot my baby?"

"I'm sorry and I'll have it fixed. I'll get hold of the gypsy; he'll fix it."

"What, that thief?"

"Don't worry; I'm paying for this, so calm down."

"But you shot my baby!"

"My God, Midge, the damned thing is twenty years old."

"I know, but Otto bought it for me," she said sadly.

"Come on, let's go home. Have a couple of beers and you'll feel better."

"I can't bear to look at it," Midge protested.

"Don't worry. I have it covered with a blanket so you won't see it," Frankie said sympathetically.

* * * * *

It was never hard to find the gypsy. He had a way of showing up when there was money to be made. Frankie waited for him outside the store. She never knew what the feud between Midge and the gypsy was about, but it was known that they were bitter enemies. Frankie spotted him coming up the street, riding an old three wheeler bike with a wooden box hooked to the rear like a trailer. He pulled up near the van.

"Hey, Frankie," he greeted her. "Good to see you're out."

Frankie opened the passenger door and pulled back the blanket that hid the hole in the seat.

"Can you fix it?"

"It's a piece of cake, as long as I don't have to do business with her majesty." Frankie just shook her head in amazement over how two grown people could act

Like babies.

"No, you deal with me, and I'll pay you, so you don't have to go near her, okay?"

"Now remember. I'm doing this for you, not her," the

37

gypsy said, pointing at the window.

She wanted to see Doc again. Maybe he could help her, because this thing didn't make any sense. Why was everyone so scared to talk? Doc was the only one she felt she could turn to. If he couldn't find out, no one could. Frankie didn't know much about the robbery. She would have to find out how they did it. They had managed to get into one of the most highly guarded buildings in the diamond center. The part that amazed her was that nobody in this city would even suspect Doc of having enough brains to figure a job as intriguing as this was. *I guess even Doc had his brilliant moments.* The irony of the whole thing was that in spite of all she had done to protect her brother, he wound up dead anyway. Doc was right about him. If he had been caught, he would have fingered all of them to save himself.

Frankie walked into the cleaner's. Midge was sitting at the counter, still sulking. "I'm leaving now; I'll be back in about three hours. See you later."

Frankie walked over to Midge and put a comforting arm over her shoulders. "Listen. Your baby will be good as new when the gypsy finishes. Now stop sulking. See you later."

* * * * *

It seemed odd that the poolroom was almost empty at nine o'clock in the morning. There were always a few losers hanging around, even this early. Frankie walked to the back and ran into Theo, standing in his usual spot with his arms folded. "Nice to see you again, little lady."

"I want to talk to Doc."

"Wait here," he said, and let himself into the office. A few seconds later the door opened and Theo waved her in. "Go on in."

Doc sat at his desk counting several stacks of money.

"Hi, sweetheart. What can I do for you?"

Frankie walked into the office and sat down, not as confident as she had been before. "Look, Doc, I hate to bother you, but you're the only one I can trust. I want you to see what you can find out for me, plus get that parole officer off my back."

Doc stopped counting and looked up at her. "I already tried, I told you that. The town is closed down tight. If there were any answers I'd know by now. And I'll take care of your parole officer, now go home and don't worry."

"Try one more time, please."

Doc lit up a cigar. "On one condition," he said sternly. "If I can't find anything out this time, you drop this nonsense about your brother and get on with your life."

Frankie was silent.

"Well, is it a deal?"

"Yes, it's a deal," she said reluctantly."

"Now go home and don't worry."

Frankie started to walk out, then stopped in her tracks. She looked him directly in the eye. "How did you do it Doc?"

"Do what?"

"The robbery. How did you pull it off?"

"Sit down and I'll tell you."

CHAPTER THREE

THE ROBBERY

Doc seemed composed now. "You have to understand this took me months of planning before I picked the people I wanted." Doc paused to get two bottles of beer out of the refrigerator and handed a bottle to Frankie. Then he continued, "I knew that Global Enterprises on occasions fenced hot diamonds for the mob. So, I went there with some diamonds I bought off a dealer I know. I went there pretending to sell the hot diamonds. I refused their offer three times, so each time I went I could case the place. I knew I was pushing it going back three times, but I had to take the chance. What I found out was very interesting. Supposedly, the most heavily guarded diamond exchange was a sham; six of the cameras were fake or not working. Their alarm system was an old antique." Doc started laughing; he got two more beers, and, handing one to Frankie, he continued, "I sold them the diamonds, then left. I sat on the information for almost a year, then I picked four people I could trust. I took care of the wiring myself. Frankie, you wouldn't believe how easy it was. We came in through the skylight on the roof. We blew the safe, and the rest is history. Well, now you know the whole thing."

Frankie stood up, saying, "Doc, my hat's off to you. You made it sound simple, but I don't think anyone else ever would have had the nerve to pull it off."

Frankie started to leave but stopped again. "One more thing Doc."

"What now?" he said, trying not to sound annoyed.

"Why wasn't I in on this job?" Doc just said, "Your brother

did not want you in."

"I'll take care of Jack Wise for you," he called out as Frankie got to the door. She turned for a second and simply said, "Thanks, Doc, I knew I could depend on you."

Doc waited until he felt it was safe to make his call, and then pressed the button under his desk floor with his heel. Theo came in. "Yes, boss what is it?"

"Theo I don't want to be disturbed for now."

"Ok, boss," he said, closing the door. Doc dialed a number and the phone rang four times on the other end. He could hear the beep and a recording came on. "Yo, this is Arty; I ain't in now. So when you hear a beep, leave a message."

Doc was frustrated now. "Call me when you get home. There is a change in plans."

Doc buzzed Theo again. "Yea boss."

Doc looked at him for a second, and then changed his mind. "Forget it," he said. Doc had decided not to take any action against Frankie, considering she had decided to leave town, so he would give her enough money to settle somewhere else, maybe L.A. By the time she got wise, he would be long gone. Now, if he could get hold of Arty to tell him to hold off…if he could not find Arty in time, he would go to plan B.

* * * * *

Frankie stood in front of the pool hall looking around to see if her pursuers were hiding in the shadows. She decided to walk part way back to the cleaners. She wanted to try and think this problem out; Frankie thought the walk would help. She knew this city, and it would not give up its secrets easy; somewhere, somehow, someone has to know something. *Could it be that no one knows because it's the work of one person and he's not telling anybody? Maybe it's time to forget this mess, take the money and move on with my life.*

They were on her before she knew it. Two men in ski masks jumped her. One of them punched her in the ribs as they dragged her into the alley. Frankie tried to fight back, but the punch weakened her. The taller of the two men clasped his arms between her shoulders and neck, while the shorter man grabbed her by the jacket and dragged her further into the alley, where he slammed her up against a garbage dumpster and put a knife to her throat. Frankie tried to break free, but his grip was too strong. The bigger man let her loose, hitting her in the face. The force of the blow knocked her back against the dumpster and she fell over.

Grabbing her jacket collar, the taller man lifted her off the ground, and when he did, Frankie noticed his tattoo. Behind the ski mask, she could see a pair of cold, steel blue eyes.

"I want you to listen to me real good," he hissed in her face. "You're asking a lot of questions that are making some of my friends nervous. They want you to stop. In fact, they want you out of the city, understand? This time it's only a warning!"

Frankie spit in his eyes. "You think you're a big man now, huh?" She tried to struggle free, but he held on to her jacket.

The shorter man laughed and pushed the knife back up against Frankie's throat, applying enough pressure on the blade that he could see a trickle of blood. "We're not supposed to kill you, but I want you to bleed a little so you understand this is no joke."

He backed away and suddenly slammed a fist into the side of her face. Frankie's head jerked back and blood spouted from her nose. The pain sent her orbiting and she felt herself starting to lose consciousness. One more blow like that and she thought she'd be dead.

"That's it, stupid!" the taller man shouted. "You want to kill her?" He grabbed Frankie by the hair and the shorter man let go.

When Frankie fell to the ground, they took turns kicking her. "You better kill me, because I'm going to kill you both when I catch you!" was the last thing she remembered saying before she lost consciousness. She felt her body lift into the air, floating on a cloud of darkness that slowly pushed her into the light. Frankie could feel the sunlight and cool water gently flow over her as she drifted along with the current. In the distance, she could see an island, its white sand gleaming in the sun. Jason was on the beach waving to her. He called out her name and she sat up. The cloud gently dropped her onto the beach and she felt the warm sand beneath her feet. Jason was coming toward her, waving. But she could no longer understand what he was saying. Doc was holding him back, pulling him away from her. She thought she yelled out her brother's name, but no sound came out of her mouth.

* * * * *

Frankie opened her eyes. She was lying in the alley in a puddle of water from a heavy rain that had turned into a drizzle. An old man with a raggedy plaid blanket draped over his shoulders was kneeling over her, shaking her. "Lady, hey, lady," he shouted in her ear, "Are you all right?"

Frankie sat up, trying to shake the cobwebs from her head.

"This is my alley," the old man told her, pointing a finger at himself. "If you want, you can stay here tonight, but not forever. There's only room for one person."

The old man tried to help her up, but she was too weak and dizzy and her sides felt like they were caving in. She squinted up at the sky through bruised eyes and could see that it had turned pitch black. She held her wrist up and looked at her watch --- the crystal was broken and the minute hand was gone. Frankie tried to lift herself up, but her head started to spin. She fell back down again in a heap.

"Lady, you have to go; you don't look good. You can't get sick in here. There's no one to take care of you. Let me help you find your own alley. I was here first," he said in his raspy voice.

Frankie's dark hair was stringy and wet and her face was caked with dried blood. Her clothes were soaked and clinging to her beaten body. She could barely pull herself up, but she managed to walk out of the alley holding onto the old man. She shivered, and he offered her his blanket. "I only have this one blanket. If you promise to give it back, you can wear it."

Frankie took it gratefully. She hurt all over. She could feel that her face was swollen and knew her ribs were cracked. With all the blows she'd taken to the head, it was a wonder she was still alive. She asked the old man to get her a cab; there was no way she could make it home alone. The old man tried to hail a cab, but no one would stop for him.

"What's your name?" Frankie whispered through swollen lips.

"Bob. Bob's my name."

Digging into her shoulder bag. Frankie pulled out a twenty-dollar bill. "Here, you can have this if you get me home. When we get there, I'll give you another twenty. You can buy all the blankets you want. In fact, I'll give you a brand new one."

He eyed the twenty with suspicion. "Okay, show me the way." He took the twenty and stuffed it into his shoe, then let Frankie lean on him as they shuffled to the closest bus stop.

"Bob, dig into my bag and get some change for the bus."

Bob eyed her again. "Are you sure lady?" Frankie nodded.

Bob scooped some coins out of Frankie's wallet, and when the bus arrived helped her on to the bus and to a seat. Then giving the driver the fare, sat down next to her.

He said concerned, "You're not going to keep my blanket, are you, lady?"

"No, I'm not going to keep it, Bob. I told you I would give you a new one," Frankie said, finding it hard to speak. She felt dizzy.

"And the other twenty you promised lady?"

"Yes, Bob. You can have the other twenty. I promise."

* * * * *

Midge was watching television when she heard someone pounding on the door. The sudden noise startled her.

"Who's there?" she yelled out. The voice on the other side of the door was muffled.

"I said who's there?"

Frankie leaned on the door and Bob called out again. The old man was still pounding on the door when Midge looked through the peephole. She opened the door and Frankie fell into her arms. The old man snatched his blanket from Frankie's shoulders as well as the twenty-dollar bill and ran down the hall to the steps.

"My God, Frankie? What happened?" Midge cried out, pulling Frankie into the hallway. She kicked the door with one foot and propped Frankie up on the hallway bench. Frankie slumped against the wall and fell over.

"Oh, God. Frankie you're not dead, please don't be dead," Midge wailed, taking Frankie's face in her hands. She then half dragged and half carried Frankie to the bedroom, and laid her on the bed.

Midge didn't bother to undress her, just covered her with a blanket. "My, God, what happened to you?" she asked out loud, rushing to the telephone.

* * * * *

Midge was sitting in a chair by her bed when Frankie awoke. "Thank God, you're awake. I thought you were dead last night, and who was that crazy old man? Did either of you get the name of the truck that hit you?"

Frankie tried to smile, but her mouth hurt too much. She pulled herself up into a sitting position, but still felt dizzy.

Midge jumped up and held her down by her shoulders. "You're not getting up. Not yet. I have a doctor friend coming over to look at you first."

Frankie didn't argue about it; she hurt too much. "I didn't know you knew any doctors."

"Well, he is going to be a doctor some day, so I let him practice his anatomy on me," Midge said with a laugh.

"I smell like hell. I have to take a shower."

"No shower. Not now, anyway. I think you have some broken ribs."

Frankie lay motionless. "Then a bath. If you promise to just soak. Please?" Midge begged. "Okay, I was afraid I might hurt you if I to took your clothes off last night."

Midge helped Frankie remove her clothes trying to be as gentle as possible.

Frankie was glad to get out of her bloody clothes. Midge helped her into the tub.

"Make it as hot as you can get it," Frankie urged. She laid her head back and closed her eyes, trying to forget what had happened to her. But the scenes kept playing in her head. Startled by Midge's touch, Frankie covered her face. "No!" she yelled.

"It's just me, honey. Just trying to help you out of the tub and get you back into a pair of pajamas."

The bell rang, and Midge's face brightened "It must be

him," she said, giving Frankie a happy smile.

Frankie grinned. "Are you sure you didn't have me beat up just so you could see this guy again?"

Midge looked at her a second then waved her hand. "No, silly goose," she said with a laugh. She patted her patient on the hand, then turned and ran out of the bedroom. Frankie could hear her footsteps hurrying down the hall to the front door. Muffled sounds of welcoming kisses drifted into Frankie, and then the intern walked in with his black bag and red lipstick all over his face. He was of medium height and had curly red hair. *Not bad*, Frankie thought approvingly. *I didn't know Midge had acquired such good taste in men.*

"Hello. You must be Frankie," he said, looking her over. Frankie nodded.

"Well, let's take a look at you. My name is Dustan." He smiled kindly, and then pulled the covers down to Frankie's waist. He prodded her abdomen and she winced. His hands moved to her rib cage and he touched both sides gently. Frankie let out a yell. "Yes they're broken," he said. He lifted her top and held her left breast, checking the sides and feeling their firmness. Then he pulled her top down.

"Is she all right?" Midge asked.

"She will be," Dustan said, shaking his head. "There's no internal bleeding." Turning back to Frankie, he checked her face and head for any fractures. "The swelling will go down in a few days. Put some ice on the swollen areas. And you have a couple of broken ribs. I'll wrap them in a second."

Frankie looked at him. "You can tell all this by fondling my breast?" she spat at him. Dustan's face reddened. "I was checking for bruises. You might have gotten hit there."

"Well, Dustan, that feel was free. The next one will get your fingers busted," she chided.

Midge put her hands on his shoulders, saying playfully,

"She's only kidding."

"Somehow I don't think so," he muttered. "I'm going to leave you some medication for the pain and give you something to make you sleep. You're going to need plenty of rest for the next few days. I'll stop by next week sometime."

Dustan wrapped Frankie's ribs and he put two bottles on the night table telling her that one was for pain and one had sleeping pills in it, winking at her before he left. Frankie smiled giving him the finger.

Frankie popped a pill and tried to fight the sleep at first, but fatigue won out. The last thing she heard before closing her eyes was Midge saying: "Come on, doc, I'll pay you, or you can take it out in trade."

She heard them laugh, and then the front door slammed. Her sleep was not a restful one. The beating crowded her dreams. Frankie woke herself up screaming and found Midge at her side, wiping the perspiration from her brow with a damp washcloth.

"Honey, you have got to give up this insane idea about your brother. Look what it's doing to you. I can give you some cash to leave town for a while."

"I can't, Midge. I wish I could, but I can't. I'm responsible for what happened to him."

"No, you're not. No matter what you did, you couldn't stop what was going to happen to Jay."

"Yes, there was. There had to be some thing I could have done."

"Frankie, I hope you know what you're doing," Midge cautioned, patting her face dry with the washcloth.

"Midge, I'm sorry if I ruined your night with your boyfriend."

"Oh, him. I threw him out hours ago. Try to get some sleep." Midge turned before leaving the room. "You know, I think maybe you need a little bit. I think it would calm you down. I can fix you up," Midge said playfully.

"No thanks. I can get my own when I'm ready." Frankie took another sleeping pill then and dozed off.

A little while later, Midge looked in on Frankie. She liked to tease her about men. Despite all her bravado, Frankie had always been shy around men, probably because her father had always been so hard on her. She had taken many a strapping for being in trouble, and most of that had come because she was protecting her brother. She had bragged a few times about having sex with guys, but Midge knew she was lying. Midge knew her better then her parents did.

* * * * *

The next week passed slowly for Frankie. She would have to convince everyone that she was putting this matter about her brother behind her; and that the two mugs that dragged her into the alley had scared her enough to make her leave. She had Midge go the library to get copies of the old newspapers about the robbery, then go down to the alley to find Bob and give him his new blanket. Midge was the only one she trusted.

The swelling on her face had gone down a little and her sides still hurt, but she was up and around. She wasn't sure she could stay cooped up in the apartment another week, but it was important for her enemies to think she had given up. It was 3 p.m. by the kitchen clock and she knew Midge would be home in three hours. Frankie hoped Midge had the information she needed. However, the more information she got, the more questions that had to be asked.

Doc wasn't clever enough to pull the robbery off alone. Could he have had some inside help? That was possible. Just thinking about it made Frankie tired. She lay back against the pillows, closed her eyes and fell into a restful sleep for the first time in a week.

* * * * *

Midge had left the cleaners early to go to the library to find the information Frankie wanted. It had taken her a few hours to do the research and then make her blanket delivery. Frankie told her to take a couple of books out just in case she was being followed. Midge thought it was a silly idea. Who would waste their time following *her*? As far as anyone knew, she didn't know anything. But she went ahead and did it anyway. She had just folded the photocopied news articles and tucked them between the pages of the book she was taking out, when two men appeared at her side. "Well, fancy meeting you here," the taller of the two said.

Midge jumped. "Artie, you scared the hell out of me."

"This is Benny, my partner," he said, nodding his head in the shorter man's direction. "What are you doing in the library?"

"I could ask you the same thing," Midge said defensively.

"Just showing my friend here the sights. You know how these out-of-towners are. By the way, how's Frankie doing?" Artie asked.

"She's doing fine."

"I am glad she decided to leave town. She could really get hurt next time."

"How did you know what happened to her?" Midge was suspicious now.

"You know how these things get around." Artie grinned.

"Yeah, I guess you're right."

"Well, give Frankie my regards. See you around."

"May I take a look at your book?" Benny asked out of the

blue. "I'm a big reader myself." He reached out and took the book from Midge.

Midge was startled by the request, but even more by the tattoo on his hand. It was the same one Frankie had described to her.

* * * * *

Frankie felt Midge shaking her. "Wake up, Frankie. Wake up."

Frankie turned reluctantly and opened her eyes. She groaned groggily, but the look on Midge's face told her something was up.

"What's wrong?"

Midge started pacing the floor. "You will never guess who I met in the library. I think I know who beat you up."

Frankie looked at her in amazement. She had never seen Midge so agitated.

"Slow down. Tell me what happened."

Midge took a deep breath, and then told about her meeting with Arty and Benny and seeing Benny's tattoo. Frankie started to get excited.

"I knew someone would slip up! Help me up," she said, stretching her arms out to Midge.

Midge helped her limp out to the kitchen table, then handed her the book with photocopies in it. "I'll put on some coffee and send out for Chinese."

* * * * *

As they ate, Frankie and Midge took turns reading the copies. "I don't know about the other guy, but Artie worked for Doc," Midge said.

"Yeah, but why would Doc want to hurt me?"

"That's what we need to find out," Midge said, looking Frankie in the eyes. "Frankie, I know how you feel about Doc. But if he has enough pull to get Jack Wise off your back, he has to have some heavy friends to make a sleaze like Wise jump through a hoop."

Frankie thought about what Midge said. It made sense. There wasn't much in the papers about the robbery, outside of what she already knew.

What was the connection between the robbery and the drugs? Was Jason really dealing? If she could find that connection, she would have the murderer of her brother.

"You may be right, but if I accuse Doc of anything and I'm wrong, then I lose the only friend out there who can help me."

"Look, Frankie, all I'm saying is look at this with an open mind. Forget for now that Doc is your friend."

"Suppose there was something else in the safe besides the diamonds. Drugs, money, or maybe there were more diamonds in the safe then they wanted to admit," Frankie said, pausing to take a sip of her coffee.

"If it were drugs, Doc would have known that I would have stopped Jay from selling them, so maybe he needed me out of the way."

"Now you're using your head, but how do we find that out?"

"There is no 'we.' This is my problem. I don't want you to get hurt on account of me, so you're out of this."

"That's a load of crap. I told you before I'm in this thing with you, whether you like it or not!" Midge replied stubbornly.

Frankie relented. "Okay, but on one condition --- you do exactly what I say and no more."

"You got it, baby," Midge said, doing her best Humphrey Bogart imitation.

"The first thing to do is find out where these two punks live without anyone getting suspicious, and that's going to be your job. Then we'll pay them a little visit."

"Unless he moved, I know where Artie lives. I was there once," Midge said thoughtfully. She caught Frankie's eye. "Don't look at me like that! It was a social visit. Besides, in case you didn't know it, he's gay. So I'm thinking Benny is, too."

Frankie shook her head. "Midge, I said it before and I'll say it again, you never cease to amaze me." Both women laughed.

"Tomorrow, I'm going to see Doc and tell him I'm going to rest up a couple of weeks and leave for California. I'll send him my address so he can mail me what he owes me."

"I never asked. How much does he owe you?"

"Midge, remember, curiosity killed the cat."

"I see. You're getting that much?"

Frankie looked at her friend. "When the time comes, I'll tell you. Right now I can't."

"You mean you don't trust me?"

"If I didn't trust you, you wouldn't be helping me, so cut the crap and admit you're just too damned nosey. Besides, what you don't know you can't tell."

Midge stuck her tongue out at Frankie and left the kitchen.

* * * * *

Before running her morning errands, Midge dropped Frankie off at the pool hall. Frankie hobbled in, putting on an act. She was still sore, but she wanted Doc to think she was still in bad shape. She reached the office door and Theo greeted her in his usual manner. "Hello, little lady. Heard what happened to you. Doc's waiting for you inside."

"Thanks, Theo," she said, walking as if in pain.

Doc was at her side the minute she entered the room, and helped her to a chair. "I heard what happened to you. I got my boys out looking. We'll find them"

"Don't bother, Doc," Frankie began. "I've been thinking that you were right. It took almost getting my brains knocked out to make me realize it. I think I need a few more weeks to rest up. At the end of the month, I'm out of here. I have some relatives in California. I'll send you an address where you can send my money."

Doc looked at Frankie sympathetically. "You're doing the right thing, kid. Your money will get to you when the time is right." Reaching into his top desk drawer, he took out a white envelope. "Here. Take this. You're going to need it for a fresh start. No payback necessary." He stood up and kissed her forehead.

"Thanks, Doc. This means a lot to me. You didn't have to do it." Frankie stood up and Doc helped her to the door. Midge and the van were waiting outside and Midge helped her into the passenger seat.

"How did it go?"

"Not bad; he bought the whole story. He even gave me this." Frankie opened the white envelope and started counting. When she finished, she put the bills back in the envelope.

"Well, damn it. Aren't you going to tell me how much?" Midge asked.

"Twenty-five thousand. If he *is* guilty, it's a cheap price to pay to get rid of me."

"Did he have the money waiting for you? Like he knew you were going to leave?"

"Yes, but that doesn't prove anything."

"I still don't trust him," Midge said, starting the engine. "The two guys who beat you up work for him."

"I guess we'll find out sooner or later." Frankie said, yawning.

Frankie was feeling a little tired. She laid her head back against the seat and tried to digest Midge's words. *If Midge is right, I won't ever get a chance to spend any of this money. I know it looks bad, but not Doc.*

A few minutes later, the van came to a stop and Frankie opened her eyes. They were home.

"You don't look good, Frankie. But don't worry, a few beers and you'll sleep like a log," Midge said cheerfully.

CHAPTER FOUR

THE SILENT CITY

It seemed to Frankie that the more questions that were answered the more confusing things got. Everything pointed to Doc, but she had no real proof. Maybe it was because she didn't want to believe that Doc would have her brother killed, or, for that matter, have anyone try to hurt her. Maybe Midge was right about Doc. But it seemed that Artie was the key. She knew she would need to talk to the people involved in the actual robbery.

"I want to talk to the guys involved in the diamond heist," Frankie told Midge.

"Before we go any further, we need to get something straightened out between us."

"What's wrong?" Frankie asked.

"You have fed me bits of information about this affair and I think I got the whole thing figured out. But either you trust me enough to tell me the whole story, or you don't. If I were going to betray you, I would have already done it."

"It's not that," Frankie said in protest, getting only an icy stare from Midge.

"Okay, so maybe I didn't trust you completely," she admitted.

"After all I've risked helping you; I think you owe me some answers."

"You're right, and I'm sorry but you know you have never been able to keep a secret."

"Are you calling me a big mouth?" Midge said, sounding hurt.

"Yes". Frankie said flatly. "Want some examples?"

"Well, I've changed, and besides, this is too serious a matter for that kind of silliness."

Frankie opened the refrigerator and pulled out two beers. She handed one to Midge and motioned to her to sit. It was time she told her the whole story. Frankie sat across the table from Midge and twisted the cap off her bottle. She took a long sip, sat back in her chair and began by telling Midge why she had taken the rap for her brother and why her parents blamed her for her Jason's death. She told Midge about how Doc had not given her share of the money. Midge had figured out most of what Frankie had told her, but was amazed at the actual amount of money involved. And now they knew one thing for certain --- they wouldn't be able to get near Artie and Benny without Doc becoming suspicious.

"Look, I have a friend who would help us out."

"Are you sure that this friend would help?"

"She has her price, but she'll help."

"Whatever it is, I'll pay it, but I need to know how and where you met her, because I know all your friends, you know that." Frankie grinned.

"Make a pot of coffee," Midge ordered. "I'll call her and ask her to come over and she can tell you herself, Miss Never Trust a Friend. "

* * * * *

Karen Holmes sat at the kitchen table. Her long black hair was parted down the

Middle and covered both sides of her sad face. Frankie had grown weary listening to all

The small talk, and decided to jump in and be blunt.

"Why are you willing to get mixed up in all this? And what's your price?"

Karen looked at Midge, who nodded in approval, and Karen started to unbutton her blouse. Staring straight ahead and not looking at either of them, she told her story in an unemotional monotone voice. Three years ago, she had been at a party with her boyfriend Eric, when Artie and Benny showed up.

"They were both high on something. Artie came over to me and grabbed my arm and started to drag me away from Eric. Eric hit Artie and knocked him down." Karen removed her blouse and revealed a once perfect breast pocked with cigarette burns and cuts. Her chest and abdomen were burned and scarred. Frankie turned away, feeling nauseous. "Artie and Benny had stuck a knife in Eric's back, and then kicked him until they thought he was dead.   Now he's stuck in a wheelchair for life," Karen said, wiping the tears from her cheeks. Midge got up and returned from the bathroom with a box of tissues. "Everyone at the party left the house," Karen told them, "and nobody tried to help us. They were even too frightened to call the cops. Everyone took off without so much as calling an ambulance. Artie and Benny had dragged me into a bedroom and tortured me for what seemed like an eternity. Midge found me wandering the streets and took care of me till I was better. If it weren't for her, I would have died," Karen said, tears running freely down her cheeks.

"Don't look away, look at me!" Karen pulled back the hair from both sides of her face, revealing two jagged scars etched deeply into her cheeks. Frankie gasped and looked away. Midge had seen Karen's face before, but she still felt sick.

"Those bastards, those rotten bastards!" Frankie's voice quivered. "Name your price. I'll pay it!"

"My price is that I want to make them pay for what they

did to me and Eric," Karen said, buttoning her blouse up. "I want to do to them what they did to me."

"They're yours when I finish with them," Frankie said, pounding her fist on the table.

"Yes, I've waited a long time for this day," Midge interrupted. "But first we need a plan, dear ladies."

"These two bastards are killers! So whatever plan we come up with is going to have to be a good one." Frankie sat back and stroked her chin thoughtfully. "We know where they live. And we know that they usually get home at about one-thirty in the morning when nothing's going on, so getting into the apartment is easy."

Midge refilled everyone's cup. "If anything happens to those two, Doc is going to suspect you, Frankie," she said, stirring a teaspoon of sugar in the coffee. "I have to come up with something good. Frankie, all you have to do is comb your hair the same way as Karen does and you two look nearly alike. Karen's only a bit taller, but who's going to notice? She takes the plane to California and we do in those scum buckets."

"Remember your promise. I get them after you," Karen pointed out.

"Don't worry. I know a place we can chain them up in until you get back," Midge said, reaching out to pat Karen's hand.

"Look, it's getting late and I'm tired. We can plan this out better tomorrow. I'm beat. Karen, stay here for tonight. You can stay in the spare room," Midge offered.

Karen started to object and Frankie interrupted. "You may as well do it or she'll never let you hear the end of it," she said with a big grin.

* * * * *

A month had passed since Frankie last talked to Doc. The

swelling on her face had gone down and her ribs were nearly healed. But Frankie had decided to keep up the pretense of still being badly injured.

The plan was simple. On Thursday, the last day of the month, Frankie would have her hair blown out straight at a salon so she could pass for Karen, if anyone were watching. Then Midge would drive her to JFK where Karen would be waiting for her in a ladies' room they had chosen beforehand. They would be dressed alike. Karen looked enough like Frankie to board the plane. If anyone was watching, they would never know the difference. Karen would fly on to L.A., and then take the 'red eye' back to New York. Meanwhile, Frankie would return to the city to an apartment that Karen had secured for Frankie. With all the players thinking Frankie was gone, Midge, Karen and Frankie would be able to set their trap. Now all they had to do was wait.

Frankie told Karen that once she reached California she would be safe. Karen would stay at a pre-arranged motel until she and Midge got in touch with her. "No one is to know you are there," she cautioned.

Frankie called Doc and told him that she had made her reservations and was getting ready to leave, but she hoped he wouldn't mind if she talked to the guys who were in on the robbery before she left.

"Maybe one of them may know something," she said hopefully over the phone.

"You could if any of them were alive," he told her. Murray had been killed in a hit and run and Louis had accidentally fallen off the roof of his building while he was tending his pigeons. And Eddie had just disappeared; no one knew where he was.

Later, Frankie told Midge what Doc had said. "Well, there it was in one neat package, three men dead, one missing."

"Things don't sound right to me." Midge paced across the living room and plopped down in her favorite armchair. "Five people commit a robbery, only two left, and one is in hiding. Do you still think your precious Doc is an innocent babe in the woods? My ass he is."

"I guess I am being stubborn, but I've known him all my life and he has always been good to me. Maybe if we find Eddie, I'll be sure of everything."

Midge threw up her hands and rolled her eyes. "Talk about a brick having to fall on your head."

"I'm sorry, but that's how I feel."

They spent the next few days asking around about Eddie; no one knew anything, or at least they weren't talking. It seemed as if they had come up against a brick wall. It wasn't until the third day that Midge got a call at the cleaners from Eddie. He had something to tell Frankie about her brother's death. He left Midge with directions to a meeting place and cautioned her to make sure that she and Frankie weren't followed.

This breakthrough boosted Midge's spirits. Midge quickly called Frankie to tell her that she would meet her at work and that they would catch something to eat on the way to the station. They had no way of knowing that Doc had their phone tapped and that Arty and Benny were at the station waiting for Eddie to show up.

* * * * *

They took the bus to Thirty-Fourth Street, weaving quickly through the hordes of shoppers. Midge spotted Eddie coming up out of the subway station at the corner of 7th Avenue. He was staggering up the stairs and fell into Midge's arms. She propped him up against the wall of a store and saw the blood dripping down the side of his mouth.

"Eddie, what's wrong?" Midge asked frantically.

Frankie held him by his left arm. He was trying to talk. "Fran.... Doc," he mumbled.

"What about Doc, Eddie?" His words were low and she put an ear close to his mouth.

"Doc.... Do...." Eddie muttered. His eyes rolled and he slid to the ground. Both women stared at him lying on the sidewalk.

"Oh my God! Midge, he's dead." Frankie felt an instant rush of adrenaline.

"Let's get the hell out of here," Midge grabbed her by the arm and pushed her through the through the throng. In the rush of people and traffic, Eddie looked like another homeless person who had fallen asleep against a wall.

They were nearly two blocks away when two men appeared and motioned for them to stop.

"Hey, we had nothing to do with that. We only wanted to talk to him," Frankie said, stepping in front of Midge.

"Senorita, I do not know or care about this problem you have. I was sent by Mister Ricardo Montoya to get you both."

"Yeah, well, we don't know any Ricardo," Midge answered, trying to regained her composure.

"It does not matter. He knows both of you, and I have been told to bring you to see him."

Frankie dug her hand into her shoulder bag, but the second man stepped forward and grabbed her arm with his right hand. He stroked his mustache. "Señorita, there is no need for that. If Señor Montoya had wanted any harm to come to you, we could have done it days ago. You can let go of that now," he said, pointing to the gun Frankie was pulling out of her shoulder bag. She let the .38 drop back to the bottom of the bag.

"What does he want with us?"

"I only know that he has invited you both to dinner and I must take you to him."

"Wait a second. I want to talk to my friend," Frankie said, grabbing Midge by the arm. The women walked off a few feet.

"What do you think? Should we make a run for it?" Midge's dark eyes were full of fear.

Frankie thought for a second. "No, let's go with them. Maybe we can find out something new. And besides, an invitation to dinner sounds good to me."

"Maybe we should bring a food taster," Midge sarcastically suggested.

* * × * *

The bar in the limo made the traffic across the Washington Bridge more tolerable. The limo turned onto Sylvan Boulevard. Neither Frankie nor Midge spoke about what had happened at the subway station. The limo turned onto a dirt road until it came to a set of large double gates covered with ivory. The driver rolled down the window and spoke into a small box. The gate opened and the limo moved slowly up the long u-shaped driveway.

Both men got out of the limo and the taller of the two opened the door for Frankie and Midge. The taller man guided then up the steps and into the house, while his companion drove away, crunching the gravel beneath the limo's tires.

The house reminded Frankie of Spanish villas she had seen in magazine photos. The man rang the bell, and after a few seconds the heavy oak door swung open. A tall slender woman in a maid's uniform answered and looked down expressionlessly at Frankie and Midge. She said nothing, and opened the door wider to let everyone in. Their escort spoke softly to the maid. She nodded and walked to the end of the open hallway to a pair of closed oak doors. The maid knocked, then slid the doors open and entered. She reappeared a few seconds later and whispered something to the man.

"Right this way please," she said, waving two fingers at Frankie and Midge. "He will see you now."

Frankie and Midge walked into the den and looked around. The walls were decorated with paintings and artifacts from Latin America and lined with several wood cabinets displaying numerous statues.

Senor Montoya was seated behind an enormous oak desk and motioned for the women to step forward. He stood to greet them, giving a quick bow. He was a tall, thin man with a neatly trimmed mustache. Aside from a small scar on his left cheek, Frankie thought he looked quite distinguished. "I trust you had an uneventful trip," he said, raising his glass of sherry to them, "and that Miguel and Antonio treated you well. I hope both of you have brought along your appetites."

"Let's cut the small talk," Frankie interrupted. "Why are we here?"

"First let us eat and then we will talk," he said pleasantly, ignoring Frankie. Ricardo Montoya pressed a button underneath his desk, and the doors again slid open. Antonio appeared and led Frankie and Midge to the dining room.

* * * * *

After a sumptuous dinner, followed by an elegant dessert of chocolate mousse, Senor Montoya suggested having coffee in the den. Frankie was the first to speak. "The dinner was great. And you're a terrific host, but why are we here? And who are you anyway?"

Ricardo Montoya laughed. "You help steal my diamonds and heroin and you act as though you are a woman of virtue."

"What the hell are you talking about?" Frankie shouted, taken by surprise. "I don't know anything about any heroin!" Frankie was starting to put two and two together, and she hoped it wasn't too late.

Midge had started to panic. "Frankie, you better straighten this thing out. I don't think I'll look good dead."

"Your friend gives you good advice. Please do as she says, as I do not wish to harm either of you," Ricardo said, taking the last sip of wine from his glass.

"We were content to wait until you got out of prison, but small amounts of our product are making their way to the street. Before we could find anything out, all activities stopped. And it has cost me quite a bit of money to get you an early release."

"You got me released?" Frankie was confused.

"Yes, my dear. You think it's a miracle that the police do not bother you? Your friend paid off your parole officer, saving me some money, but still, it was costly," Ricardo said, twirling his wine glass by the stem.

"You know Doc?" Frankie asked suspiciously.

"No, I do not deal with second rate thieves like him. I only know that he helped you out."

"I hope you're going to believe what I'm about to tell you," Frankie said.

"My dear, you will find me a very sympatric listener if you are telling the truth." Frankie took a deep breath and told Ricardo her story from the beginning, up to their meeting with Eddie that afternoon.

"I am not saying you are a liar, senorita, but as they say in your country, 'that is one hell of a whopper.'"

"Believe it or not, it's the truth," Frankie said, ready to dive across the table and grab Ricardo by the throat. "You wasted your money getting me out of prison because I don't know anything about your drugs."

"We will see." Ricardo said presently.

Ricardo pressed a button under the table. Seconds later, the maid came, in followed by Miguel and Antonio. He gestured with one hand to Frankie and Midge. "Maria, they will be spending the night with us as our guests. Please have Pilar show them to their rooms."

"You mean your prisoners, don't you, Señor? Frankie felt her blood rush.

"No, Senorita. I said guests," Montoya said pleasantly.

"I know how it sounds. If you give me some time, I can prove it," Frankie insisted.

"I will make some inquires. If you are telling the truth, I will give you the chance you desire. For now, my house is your house." He pushed his chair back from the table, bowed to the women and left the room without another word.

* * * * *

Frankie looked around the bedroom, admiring the exquisite antique furniture and framed artwork on the walls. This bedroom, and the entire house, or at least what she had seen of it, was furnished in the way she had only seen in magazines and in the movies. She bounced on the bed a little, liking the feel of the down comforter and the soft pillows. At least she'd sleep well tonight.

She jumped when the door opened. It was Midge. "Want a joint?" She pulled one out from under her rolled up sleeve and gave a low whistle. "I hope we live long enough to see the rest of this place." Then she changed her tone. "I told you that fat slob was responsible for your brother's death. And everything else that has happened to you."

"Okay, so you were right. Things are starting to make sense

now."

Frankie jumped up and put her hands to her face. "How could anyone have known we were going to meet Eddie? I don't know how anyone could have, unless you opened your mouth!" Frankie said accusingly.

"Hey!" Midge yelled. "I didn't say anything to anyone, I swear."

"I'm sorry. This thing has me rattled."

Frankie walked over to the window and pulled back the curtains. She stared out into the courtyard below. "Isn't Ricardo dreamy?" she said wistfully.

"Midge, in all honestly, I think he's the most handsome man I ever met," Frankie said with a little excitement in her voice.

Midge laughed. "You sound like a school kid with her first crush."

Frankie was embarrassed and her face reddened. Midge winked and sang out, "Frankie's in love, Frankie's in love."

The last thing Midge heard as she shut the door was Frankie's shoe slamming into it.

* * * * *

Ricardo Montoya sat at his desk, pondering Frankie's story. He had been quite taken by her. She stirred up feelings in him that he had not had in many years. He wanted to get to know her better, but he wanted to be sure she was not lying to him in order to gain his trust. All through their discussion in the office, things had not gone the way he expected. He hoped she was telling the truth. He had watched her every gesture when she talked. Her cleft chin added to her dark beauty. He had the feeling that she could take care of herself, but some of her toughness was just an act to keep people away.

* * * * *

Frankie was awakened by a knock on the door. "Señorita, are you awake?" the maid asked pleasantly.

Frankie yawned and stretched. "Yes I am."

Pilar smiled and walked in with Frankie's clothes, neatly hung on a wooden hanger.

"What are my clothes doing on a hanger?"

"Señor Montoya thought you would feel refreshed with clean clothes so I had them cleaned and ironed," the maid replied. "I will draw your bath and breakfast will be served at nine o'clock." Pilar moved across the room to the adjoining bathroom and Frankie could hear the water running.

Nothing like being clean and well-fed before you get knocked off, she thought wryly. She got out of bed and padded across the floor to the bathroom. Pilar curtsied and left the room, shutting the door gently behind her. Frankie stripped off the nightgown that had been left on her pillow the night before and eased into the tub. The warm soapy water was relaxing and she rested her head against the softness of the bath pillow left by the maid. Through half-closed eyes, Frankie admired the gold fixtures and the marble tiles. *I could really get used to this type of life. When, that is, if I get my money this is the way I want to live. Yes indeed, this is the life.*

* * * * *

Midge was already at the breakfast table when Frankie arrived. "This is the life," she whispered good-naturedly to Frankie as she slid into the seat next to Midge.

Ricardo Montoya walked in off the patio just as they started to have their morning meal --- an elaborate presentation of eggs, toast, pancakes, sausage, fresh fruit, coffee and juice.

"Señoritas, I trust everything was satisfactory this morning," he said, taking a seat. Pilar poured him some coffee. "I am sorry that I could not join you, but I have some good news for you both. My men located the porn broker who turned your brother in to the police. He was a little reluctant to talk; however, Miguel has a way with people. After a little coaxing, he was more than willing to talk about the events. And it seems that you were telling the truth about how you got caught. So I must assume that you are telling the truth about not participating in the robbery. The men you say actually committed the robbery are indeed dead. Either that is a coincidence or someone wants to keep everything for themselves."

Frankie interrupted him. "Look, I told you what happened. Someone owes me money for serving time, and that someone is Doc Murdock," she said angrily.

Montoya smiled at the women. "My problem is this: I believe you were not in on the actual robbery, but there is nothing to tie Doc Murdock into any of this, except your word. Everyone you say was in on the robbery is dead and you say it is my problem. That bothers me. How do I know that this is not some sort of set-up between the two of you? I want to believe you, so I am going to give you time to get me my twenty-five kilos of heroin. And. by the way, it was ninety million, not sixty million in diamonds. Miguel and Antonio will be at your disposal if you need them."

"It's your stuff; you get it back," Frankie snapped.

"The insurance company has paid me for the diamonds. I could not account for the drugs for reasons you can well understand. You get my property back and I will give you the money you are owed, plus a bonus. Or you can have the diamonds and they're yours to do with as you wish. You understand I cannot get involved in this matter because of my stature. It may look suspicious."

"Well, my dear Señor Montoya, we need to make a deal, or no dice."

"What is it you propose?"

"We need to talk in private," Frankie demanded. Excusing himself and Frankie from the table, Ricardo escorted her into his office. Ricardo Montoya had not looked at another woman in ten years. This one was someone he would want to see again. They talked for an hour, before reaching an agreement.

* * * * *

The ride back was a quiet one. Both Midge and Frankie were lost in their own thoughts. Frankie was giving Montoya's proposition some thought, when Midge spoke up. "You're not going to tell me what you talked about with Montoya, are you?"

"No," Frankie said flatly.

Midge sat back in the leather seat. "Why not?"

Frankie's eyes were closed. "Ricardo, I love that name." She said in a dreamy voice to Midge.

"Are you crazy? You know who he is, don't you?"

"Yes, I know who he is." Frankie sighed.

"If the people who wanted to buy your place are still interested, I think you should sell," Frankie said, as if she had not heard a word Midge had said.

"That's it? That's all you have to say?"

"For now."

"For now," Midge mimicked her. The limo moved off the bridge, slowly turning on to Thirty-Fourth Street. The limo came to a stop and the driver got out and opened the door for them.

"I hope you had a pleasant trip, ladies," he said, tipping

his hat to them.

"Well, let's catch the next bus back home," Frankie said.

"Bus, hell. After all that luxury? Were taking a cab back --- I'll pay."

"Don't tell me you're going to turn into a spoiled brat," Frankie said, laughing.

* * * * *

Frankie opened the refrigerator. "You want a beer?"

"What? No champagne?" Midge joked.

"No, my lady," Frankie said, imitating Antonio. "Only beer."

"Okay, let me have one." Midge reached out for the beer, twisted the top off and settled back in her chair. "So why aren't you going to tell me what you two talked about? You don't trust me anymore?"

"No, I'm not going to tell you, and yes, I do trust you. I promise that I'll tell you when the time is right."

"You want me to sell the cleaners, but you won't tell me why. What's going on? You're asking a hell of a lot, you know that?" Midge snapped in irritation.

"Have I ever done anything to hurt you?"

"No, I have to admit you saved my ass more times than I can remember," Midge said quietly.

"Then promise, just be patient and trust me and things will come out better than you expect."

Midge took a sip from her bottle and looked at Frankie for a few seconds, deciding what to do. "Damn, I'm in this deep; I may as well go all the way with you. As the British say, in for a penny, in for a pound." Frankie knew Midge would not back out now, even if it was just to find out what she and Montoya had talked about. In spite of a relaxing day, Frankie fell into a deep sleep on the sofa, drifting off with one thought: *Francine Montoya.*

* * * * *

The next few days were busy ones for Frankie and Midge. Their plan to trap Artie and Benny was still on, but Frankie had a slight alteration. She had not yet told Karen or Midge what she was thinking. Having access to Miguel and Antonio was a blessing. The pretext of going to the airport was no longer necessary. When the plan was ready for execution, she would tell them what they needed to know. Over the last couple of days, she had checked Ricardo's reputation with several sources and found that although his dealings were of an illegal nature, he had diplomatic immunity. He was also a man of his word, and had never gone back on a deal. She had promised to return his drugs and the diamonds. She would only keep her share as well as Jason's. If anything went wrong, Ricardo would see to it that Karen and Midge would be well taken care of.

She was afraid to tell Midge the full extent of her deal with Montoya because she knew Midge would object, only thinking that she was purposely putting her life on the line for her to have a great deal of money.

Their lives depended on secrecy. Montoya himself knew that the robbery was an inside job. He had not told Frankie simply because the man had accidentally died in a subway accident, and Ricardo felt that it would have not served any purpose.

While Midge was at work, Frankie called Karen. She had given Karen the address of a loft in Manhattan that Antonio had secured for her, and Frankie told her to pack one suitcase with just enough clothes for a week. The place had already been stocked with food. The keys to the front door, she told Karen, were hidden beneath a pipe cap protruding from the wall. All Karen had to do was loosen the cap and take out the keys. The apartment was on the second floor. There was a bed, television set and enough food to last for a while. "And don't leave the building under any circumstances," she warned.

Frankie told Karen that she and Midge would join her at the loft on the second day. As soon as Midge got home, she would let her know about their conversation. Frankie made one last phone call to Antonio to set the plan in motion.

* * * * *

Karen was standing outside the apartment door when Frankie and Midge pulled the elevator gate up and stepped out into the hallway. Karen hugged both women. "My God! I'm so glad you're here. It was scary being alone up here."

The women carried their suitcases into the apartment and set them down in the entry hallway. "Well, we're here to keep you company now," Frankie said. "By tomorrow night it will all be over."

"Now are you going to let us know what's going on?" Karen asked.

Midge chimed in. "Yes, I think now is definitely the time."

Frankie walked over to a card table, pulled out a chair and sat. "Come on. Sit down and I'll explain everything."

For Karen's benefit, Frankie started from the beginning; saving what she felt was the best part for the end. "Mister Montoya has let us borrow Antonio and Miguel."

Midge looked surprised. "Those were the two guys who took us to Montoya's place."

"Right. They'll bring those two scum-buckets here tonight. So the rest of what we were planning won't be necessary,"

Frankie said. "With Montoya's men here, we are completely out of danger. Midge, after it's over, you go home and back to work like nothing ever happened."

Midge looked unhappy.

"What's wrong now?" Frankie asked.

"I thought we were in this together?"

"We are, just let me finish what I have to say." Frankie grinned. "I talked Montoya into giving me a finder's fee. Plus mine and Jason's share for giving him back his drugs. I should wind up with about, give or take a buck, one hundred million dollars."

Both Karen and Midge were shocked.

"That's a lot of cash to be sporting around," Karen said breathlessly.

Frankie continued. "When we're finished here tonight, Karen will leave with Miguel and Antonio. By tomorrow night she will be on her way to Austria to be worked on by one of the best cosmetic surgeons in the world."

Karen gasped. "You mean all this can be fixed?" she said, putting her hands up to her face. Tears started to come. She jumped up and hugged Frankie so hard, they both almost fell over.

"What about me?" Midge asked, sulking.

Frankie laughed. "You, my dear friend, will distance yourself from me so you don't get hurt. I want you to sell the business and go to Miami and buy us a villa near the ocean. I think we all can live on the money from the diamonds forever." Frankie said, smiling.

"I knew there was some reason why I liked you," Midge joked.

* * * * *

The days moved slowly for the three women, all lost in their own thoughts and dreams about how the money would change their lives. Frankie checked her watch; it was eight fifteen. *They're late, or maybe they couldn't find them,* she thought. Then they heard the elevator motor whine as it slowly ascended and stopped at the end of the hall. Antonio lifted the gate, and Miguel pushed Artie into the loft. Artie stumbled forward and fell to the floor, looking up at the women. He stood on unsteady feet. His face was swollen and smattered with blood.

Karen walked towards him. "You hurt the poor boy," she said, her voice dripping with sarcasm. She leaned back, balanced herself, and kicked him in the groin. Artie doubled over and fell to his knees, crying out in agony. She kicked him again. Tears were streaming from her eyes. Artie fell to the floor and curled up in a fetal position. Karen screamed obscenities at him and kept kicking him, driving the toe of her boot into his chest, back, legs and groin.

Frankie pleaded with her to stop. Midge was crying. "Karen, please stop!"

Miguel and Antonio each grabbed her under one arm and dragged her away from Artie's battered body.

"Let me go, you bastards. I want to put him in his grave!"

Frankie smacked her across the face. "Calm down, damn you."

Karen was sobbing. The two men let her go and she put her arms around Frankie. "I'm sorry! I...I...I'm sorry. Seeing him again, I just lost control."

"It's okay. After we get some answers from this slime you can do what you want with him," Frankie said gently.

"Where's the other one?" Midge asked.

"Well, Señorita, he showed a great deal of resentment, and much displeasure in coming with us. So we decided that he should sleep with the angels," Miguel said.

"Señorita," Antonio cut in. "If I may suggest that you let Miguel and I speak with this animal. Tell me what you wish to know and I promise you answers. I am afraid that the young lady has too much hate in her."

Frankie didn't have to think about it. "I think you're right, Antonio. But don't kill him; it's up to her to take her own revenge."

"I understand, Señorita." Frankie told Antonio what she wanted to know. "I think perhaps the three of you should go out for a late dinner. I believe that two hours should be enough time. You will have all the answers you want when you return."

Frankie told Karen and Midge what Antonio had suggested. "It's up to you, Karen. At least he will be alive when we get back. We're all afraid that you'll kill him before he talks."

Karen stood silently for a few minutes, drawing a deep breath. "Yes, you're right; we should leave for a while."

Midge whistled with a sigh of relief. "I'm driving."

* * * * *

They decided that as long as they had access to the limo they might as well go to Chinatown to eat. There was plenty of small talk among them, but Frankie could feel the tension. It was Midge who broke the ice. "So, Karen, remind me not to get you mad at me," she said with a wink.

Karen smiled for the first time since she had seen Artie. As much as they tried to prolong going back, they had to. There were many unanswered questions with Artie needing to atone for his actions.

* * * * *

The elevator stopped and Frankie lifted the gate. Antonio and Miguel were sitting at the card table, having coffee and engrossed in conversation when the three women stepped into the loft. Both men stood up. "Ah, Señoritas, you are back already. I trust you had a good dinner," Antonio said.

"Yes we did, thank you," Frankie replied

"Well Senoritas, join us for some coffee; we have a great deal to speak about." Midge looked around. "Where did you put the slime bucket?"

Miguel pointed to the other end of the loft. "He is at the other end in the dark where he belongs, Señorita. "

* * * * *

Antonio waited for everyone to sit, and then he looked directly at Frankie. "Señorita, I am sorry to say that this dog who calls himself a man, on the orders of his boss, Doc Murdock, killed your brother. Should you wish to take revenge I do not blame you. He is also responsible for the murder of the men who actually committed the robbery. Senor Montoya will be happy to know that you did not lie to him about not committing the robbery."

Frankie stood up and grabbed the flashlight and walked to the back of the loft. Artie lay tied up on the floor, bruised and bleeding, in a puddle of his urine, pleading for mercy. Frankie screamed at him and kicked him several times. She clicked off the flashlight and returned to the card table. "You were saying?" Frankie said calmly to her companions.

Antonio spoke. "These men and your brother were killed because of the drugs and the stolen diamonds. The heroin was never disturbed. It is still intact. That is why we could not get any information. It seems that the stuff being circulated was not ours. It was just meant as a cover for killing your brother."

"So it was just a big lie to throw everyone off the track?" Midge said. She looked at Frankie. "I told you not to trust that fat tub of lard."

"It will still be up to you, Señorita, to secure Señor Montoya's property. For this, we will do whatever we can to help you," Antonio finished.

"That's okay. I can handle the rest myself."

Miguel walked over to the wall, flipped the switch, and the back of the loft lit up. All three women looked at Artie. Miguel stepped forward and lit up a cigar while Artie, now up on his knees, begged Miguel not to hit him again. He motioned to Karen to join him, and handed her the lit cigar.

"I promised you first crack at him. He's yours," Frankie said to Karen. Karen started kicking him again, taking deep breaths and plunging hard kicks with her right foot. Then she bent down and held the cigar over him, waving it in front of his eyes. She was aiming for his cheek, when she abruptly stopped. "I can't do it. I have no more anger left. If I kill him, I won't be any better then he is." She turned to Frankie. "He's yours now."

Frankie picked up a bloodied baseball bat that lay against the wall. She walked over to Artie. "You dirty bastard. You scarred an innocent woman. You crippled a good man, and you killed my brother." He covered his face as Frankie swung the bat, slamming it between his shoulders. She started to swing again but stopped. "You're right, Karen. If we kill him, we'd be on his level."

Midge took the bat from Frankie and smacked Artie on the head, then dropped the bat. They all looked at her in amazement.

"What? I should be the only one who didn't get in a lick? And, besides, he gave me a dirty look once."

They all laughed. "Señorita, what shall I do with him?"

Antonio asked.

"Put him with his friend. They deserve to be together. Please make sure he does not die easy."

"Yes, Señorita. If you will go and wait in the limo, we will be down in a few minutes to escort you to your homes."

"Well, ladies," Frankie said, "we won't be seeing each other for some time. A last drink until we meet in Miami? Midge, you know what to do. Karen, we wish you luck."

Frankie poured the champagne. They put their glasses together and drank a last toast.

CHAPTER FIVE

DOC'S DILEMMA

Robert Murdock's name, "Doc" was a nickname he had acquired because he had once studied medicine. At fifty-five years old he considered himself an astute businessman. Throughout the years, he engineered some very successful robberies, and he was content to have his peer's think of him as a small time thief. Doc was always able to choose his men wisely, and he felt that the smaller the group, the more loyal the men were. He had a way with his people, and they always went the extra mile for him. No one ever considered that he would cheat them or do them any harm. And those who knew the truth were no longer around to complain about it.

Suddenly, things started to unravel for him, and being a vain man, Doc would never admit that he had bitten off more than he could chew. He had robbed Ricardo Montoya, head of one of the biggest drug cartels, not only in Latin America, but in the tri-state area. Doc felt safe because his victim would be looking for someone on the inside to have helped with the job, when in fact, there was no one --- because Doc had made sure his contact was dead.

Four weeks had gone by since Artie and Benny had dragged Frankie into an alley and nearly beaten her to death. And now there was no sign of them. He had sent them to do a simple job of getting rid of the contact before Frankie left town. Now he wondered if Frankie had gotten back at them. Doc knew she was cunning and you could con her once, but she never made the same mistake twice. His mistake was not having them kill her the first time. Then he had planned to have

Theo take care of them. There would be no loose ends left after he took care of Theo. Then he would go to the safe house until things cooled down. He had held on to the heroin; there was no rush, and it was in a safe place. Doc would smuggle the twenty-five kilos out of the country before he left. He still had the diamonds. Later, he would sell them off a little at a time so there would be no suspicion.

But there was that old bell ringing in his head telling him that something was wrong. His intuition had saved his hide more then once, and he was willing to follow it again. It was time to move on. Doc had spent ten years setting up a new identity. When he left, no one, not even the great Montoya, would be able to find him. And just to add a twist of irony, he just might sell Montoya back his own drugs.

Doc had closed the pool hall for a few days, leaving a sign on the doors, CLOSED FOR REPAIRS. All he took from his apartment above the poolroom was his cash and other assets he had hidden. The rest was expendable. He had Theo rent a car under his own name so there would be no suspicion. Theo was waiting for Doc on the side street so he could leave the building unnoticed. They had secured a dead body some weeks ago; keeping it refrigerated till it was needed,

Doc knew nobody would miss a homeless person. He also managed to get dental X-rays of the dead man and replaced his own with them.

* * * * *

Doc sat in his recliner reading the paper, pleased with himself. He read the headlines out loud and laughed. "Mobster Dies in Fire!"

When the firefighters rummaged through his apartment after the fire, all they found was a dead body charred beyond recognition. The body was identified as a local mobster known as Doc Murdock. During the investigation, they found that the fire was of a suspicious nature and ruled it as arson and murder. Not bothering to read further, he knew it would wind up another unsolved crime.

Except for Theo, no one would ever find out he was in Vermont living in a rustic old home as retired banker, David Epstein. *Damn. I'm so good at what I do it scares me sometimes.* He knew he was lucky to find the bust of Cesar sitting in the corner of the safe. No one realized what it was made of so he took it.

* * * * *

Doc had purchased the house already furnished. With the last of his luggage moved in and everything neatly put away, Doc sat in his living room and put his feet up. He had poured himself a glass of White Label and was enjoying reading a New York *Times* piece about the fire. Everything had gone off just as he had planned, even down to the grieving relative, theatrics he felt would be a nice touch. He was officially dead. He could live a quiet life here in the boonies. That is, if he didn't have bigger fish to fry.

Theo was out shopping, but when he returned, Doc decided to send him back to the city to find Frankie and bring her back here. He would take care of her himself, then he would take care of Theo. No matter how perfect his plans were, as long as she was out there, he would never feel entirely safe. He knew Frankie. He knew that if she didn't buy his death, she would keep looking for him. She was that stubborn. She would keep digging, and if she got lucky, it could ruin everything for him. Frankie had to go, and that was all there was to it. *Hell. I've already killed four people. Two more won't make any difference,* he thought, taking the last swig of White Label from his glass.

He heard the back door slam and Theo came into the living room and handed him the newspapers. "Theo, we have a change in plans," Doc said, throwing his arm around Theo's brawny shoulders. "I want you to go back to the city and stay there until you find Frankie and then bring her here to me."

"You're not going to hurt the little lady, are you?"

Doc looked into Theo's worried brown eyes and feigned a hurt look. "No, Theo! Whatever gave you that idea? I just want to give her what she has coming to her." Doc said cheerfully.

Theo looked at him suspiciously. "I'll find her for you, but I don't want any harm to come to the little lady."

* * * * *

Frankie watched the firemen put out the last of the four-alarm fire. She was still there when they carried out what was left of Doc's body in a black zippered bag. There wasn't much you could see, the way he was all bagged up, but the thing that was most curious to her was Theo's absence. Of all the people in the world, the man who was the most devoted to him was nowhere to be seen. If Frankie was to make a bet, it would be that Doc was anywhere but in that body bag.

* * * * *

Frankie sat in Midge's kitchen and watched the fifteen-inch television with great interest. The regular program was suddenly interrupted when a newscaster came on the air and announced dramatically, "It has now been confirmed that the body has been identified by a close relative to be that of Robert (Doc) Murdock. He was known to have close Mafia ties and was owner of Snookies Pool Hall in the Bronx. Officials say an investigation into the cause of the fire indicates it was arson."

Frankie shouted at the television, "Yes, I got you now!" She had anticipated the next turn of events, so when the phone rang she was not surprised. "Yes?" she answered. "Yes, I can be there in an hour. No, I can get there on my own, Mr. Morales, no problem. I'll leave in a few minutes." Frankie hung up. *I know that bastard is still alive. The smart ass blew it. He didn't have any relatives. He was brought up in an orphanage. Where was Theo?* Frankie wondered

* * * * *

Frankie arrived at the Spanish Embassy at one o'clock. After a short wait, a woman of medium height came down the steps then stopped and looked directly at Frankie. She adjusted her glasses and said with some authority, "Señorita Frankie Rose."

"Yea, that's me," Frankie replied.

"Follow me, please."

Frankie followed the woman to the elevator. She was a bit disappointed that she had not been invited to Ricardo's house. The woman turned to her. "This way, Señorita, please." As they were walking, Frankie noticed a few strands of gray in the woman's otherwise perfectly coiffed auburn hair. *Clearly, it was time for a touch up job,* Frankie thought.

They reached a double door. "Please wait out here." A few seconds later, the door opened and the woman asked her to step inside, then she turned and left, her black pumps clicking sharply along the tiled corridor as she walked away.

When Frankie entered the room she expected to see Ricardo Montoya, but a different man stood behind the desk. "Ah, you must be Señorita Rose." Smiling, he stepped from behind the desk and Frankie noticed that he had a slight limp as he walked toward her. "I am Juan Morales, at your service. Señor Montoya sends his regrets that he could not be here. Some urgent business has taken him out of the country."

"I am sorry he couldn't make it. Please tell him I was disappointed that he was not here."

"I will be sure to do that, Señorita. "

"Then what is it you want from me?" Frankie asked.

"Señor Montoya has asked me to explain to you that in light of this Doc Murdock's recent death, your obligation to him is canceled. However, he will keep his promise to help the Señorita Karen Holms," he said.

"You may tell Mr. Montoya that I thank him for his kindness, and you can also tell him that Doc is about as dead as you are," she replied.

"I do not understand! The news on the television and the newspapers all tell the same story," he said sounding confused.

"I have known Doc Murdock all my life. He had no living relatives. The dental records and the identification were all a scam. He is alive and I am going to find him. You tell Mr. Montoya that for me."

"I will tell Señor Montoya and he will be most grateful to you for your honesty."

"Just tell him that it is just going to take a little more time, but not to worry. I'll find Doc."

Frankie knew now that Doc had been planning this disappearance from the day she had said she would take the rap, and that he never intended to pay off anyone. Instead, he had many people killed to cover his tracks. She wondered if Theo would be his next victim. For all her toughness, she knew he was a man to fear.

Juan Morales escorted her downstairs. "If there is any help I can give you in this matter, please contact me. Señorita, I can have the limo take you anywhere you wish to go." He handed her his business card.

"No, thank you. I have some things to do, plus I don't want to get used to the luxury," she said with a smile. After Frankie left the Embassy, she decided to walk for a while to sort things out in her head. *I have to admit that Doc is as slick as they come.* It was going to be hard to leave this city when all this was finished, but Frankie felt it was for the best, considering everything that had happened to her.

* * * * *

Frankie sat in the living room pondering her next move. Her plans had changed now. In a way she felt that the outcome wasn't so bad --- coming out in the open to make it easy for him to find her was a bit risky. Frankie knew that he would send someone to get her. Most likely it would be Theo. At least, she hoped so. But she would have to take that chance. Frankie figured that the only way Doc could get away with this scam was to leave the country, but to cover his trail she would have to die and Theo would be next. She had known Doc since Jason and she had burglarized an apartment in Manhattan when they needed a fence and they had heard of Doc. She had been twelve years old then. Doc gave them a fair shake for the loot. After that, they had worked for him on and off until she went to prison. Frankie also remembered the countless times she had made decisions in her life, and most of them had been wrong. She hoped she was right this time.

Frankie closed her eyes and tried to think. She remembered seeing a list he had on his desk with several names of people Doc had decided to use if necessary. She remembered him telling her not to pay attention to the list, that it was a game he was playing. She could not recall which one he decided on at that time, and the more she tried to remember, the more jumbled things got. If there was one thing Frankie knew, it was that Doc never trusted banks. Everything of any monetary value was with him. She used to tell him that he was so cheap he squeaked when he walked. He always felt that if he had to make a run for it, having everything he needed with him would make it easier to get away. There would be no paper trail and no one would ever be able to follow him.

* * * * *

Theo decided to get an early start driving back to New York, and although this was a job he had to do for Doc, it was something he would rather not do. He did not want to see Frankie get hurt. She had been through enough already. He could not say if Doc had anything to do with her brother's death, because there were a lot of things that Doc did not confide in him. He had been Doc's bodyguard for nearly twenty years, and had done a lot of underhanded things for him out of loyalty. There were times when Doc treated people on the level, but that was only when it served his purpose. Doc had picked him up in the streets when he was a young boy living in an alley with no parents. Theo had been left to fend for himself, stealing hubcaps and mugging drunks for money to buy food.

He had always been big for his age. At twelve years old, he was already six feet tall. Doc had done a lot for him. He had taken him off the streets and sent him back to school. When he asked Doc how he was going to pay him back, Doc said he could be his bodyguard. And that's exactly the role Theo had played for almost twenty years. So he would find Frankie for him out of loyalty. Doc said he was not going to hurt the little lady, which is what Theo had always called her. If he thought

Doc would hurt her in any way, Theo would have to give considerable thought to this whole idea. Meanwhile, he would do as he was told.

Theo had given a great deal of thought to not going to Europe with Doc. He had been thinking in recent months that he had enough money and stocks put away that he could go back to Jamaica, the country of his birth, find a good woman, get married and raise a family and live a life of leisure. Doc told Theo to keep his apartment because they were not going to leave the country at the same time. He had not told Doc of his decision not to meet him in Europe yet. He wanted to wait until he had found Frankie. Then he would have fulfilled his last obligation to Doc.

* * * * *

Frankie did not even consider looking for Doc. She knew the chances of *him* finding *her* were greater. Whichever way it happened, it would be all right with her. He was a greedy man, and greedy men always wanted more, and that's when they made mistakes. She had idolized Doc. He had been like a father to her, but now she knew him for what he was. He was going to find her, and not to give her the money she had coming to her, but to tie up a loose end --- her. The funny part about all this was that no matter how smart Doc thought he was he had made too many mistakes: the false relative bit and the breaking the eleventh commandment --- never try to screw Frankie out of her money. There would always be someone he would have to get rid of to cover his tracks. Sooner or later he would make another mistake and she would get him then, that is, of course, if he didn't get her first.

The first thing she decided to do was to write down all the things she could remember about their conversations. She removed a lone picture from the wall of the bedroom, and with a black magic marker she jotted down things she recalled from their talks. By six o'clock, Frankie could feel her stomach growling. She hadn't eaten all day. Backing away from the wall to look at her notations for a second, she then walked into the kitchen to see what was in the refrigerator. She sat down at the kitchen table and mused over leftover pizza and beer. She was mentally drained and decided to call it a night. Tomorrow she would forget this mess and just have a leisurely day before her head exploded. After a shower she went to bed and tried not to dream.

* * * * *

Things got too hectic. She was halfway down West Forty-Second Street when she heard him call out. "Yo, Frankie!" as he rolled up beside her on his three-wheeler. "Yo, Gypsy," she called back cheerfully. "What are you up to?"

"Got a job on Second Avenue. Hey, did you hear about the fire? They say Doc died in the fire."

"I know. I saw it on television," Frankie said, trying to act concerned.

"You know, I think I saw Doc's ghost the same day."

"I didn't know you believed in ghosts," she teased.

"Come on, Frankie. You're not going to make fun at me like everyone else. You know I ain't no dope!"

"I'm sorry, Gypsy. Tell me about it."

"Well, I was a few blocks from the George Washington Bridge at the corner, waiting for the light to change, when this car makes a turn, and there was Doc's ghost sitting in the front seat. It scared the hell out of me. I closed my eyes and made the sign of the cross, and he was gone."

"It was probably your imagination," she said quickly.

"Yeah, maybe you're right. I must have dreamed Theo too. Well, see ya, Frankie. I'll be late for my appointment if I don't hurry." Frankie watched him as he peddled off. She smiled as she turned into the door of a coffee shop, calling out cheerfully, "Coffee black and a powered doughnut."

* * * * *

Frankie sat on a bench in Bryant Park and thoughtfully sipped her coffee. *I knew he would make a mistake sooner or later, but I didn't think it would be quite so soon.*

The park reminded her of her school days when she and Jason would cut class. They would count the number of people entering the library on their walks to the Bowery, always making sure to stop in at Marty's Bar and Grill. Marty was a friend of their father's. He always gave them a lecture about playing hooky from school, and that they shouldn't be in a bar at their age. Then he would feed them lunch. She stood up, looking towards the library and counted out loud as tears streamed out from the corners of her eyes. Frankie could feel the hatred she had towards Doc for causing her brother's death, all due to his greed. She would have done anything for Doc, but now he had betrayed her trust and she wanted to kill him for what he had done.

* * * * *

Midge lay on the shaded beach chair drinking a Pena Colada. It hadn't taken her long to line up a string of male admirers with her gorgeous tan. She checked her watch. *Let's see... today is Wednesday, so I'd better get going. My date will be coming to pick me up for dinner. Tomorrow I will start to look for a place to live. Frankie will skin me alive if she finds out I'm screwing around.* Midge folded the rented beach chair and slowly walked away, sipping on her Pina Colada.

* * * * *

The drive back to New York had worn Theo out. There was no rush to find Frankie. He wasn't as stupid as people thought. Most of the people that Doc associated with thought that because of his size and weight, he was stupid. He had always liked Frankie. She treated him as an equal. He remembered when she graduated from high school and didn't have a date for the prom. He had teased her about it. "You want this big old black man to take you? Unless you're ashamed to be seen with me."

Frankie teased right back. "You're going to be the ugliest person there, but get a tux and be at my house at eight o'clock Friday night." Laughing, she added "My mom will have a heart attack when she sees you. That should teach you a lesson for being a smart ass. Don't be late." Theo smiled remembering the night at the prom. He'd had a good time. He smiled again because he found a parking spot near his apartment.

* * * * *

Theo stretched out on the bed and relaxed. The more he thought about going home, the better it sounded to him. Theo had decided to take the next two days to straighten out his affairs. He would transfer money to a bank in Jamaica and the rest he would remove from his safety deposit box and take with him.

Then he would look for Frankie. He wondered why the police weren't looking for him to ask questions about Doc's death. He immediately dismissed the thought, thinking Doc had probably paid them off.

* * * * *

In the morning, Theo called Doc to tell him that things were taking longer then he expected. But not to worry, he would find Frankie. He hated to lie, but Theo felt it was necessary this time. He was happy not having to stand by that office door day in and day out. So he felt a few days to tend to business and relax were in order. What Doc didn't know wouldn't hurt him. Somehow he felt she wouldn't be hard to find. But for now, he would enjoy his newfound freedom and have a good time.

* * * * *

Theo drove down to Midge's Cleaners and found to his disappointment that she no longer owned the place. The people who bought it did not know where Midge had gone. He spent most of the day looking for Frankie, but she always seemed to be one step ahead of him. On the fourth day as Theo came out of his apartment building, two men approached him.

"Señor, we would like you to accompany us," Miguel said. "There is someone who wishes to speak with you."

Theo stopped and looked at both men. "Suppose I don't want to go with you?"

"Then Señor, you will make our friend unhappy. And it will make us unhappy that we are unable to help our friend."

Miguel grabbed Theo's arm and tried to force him into the limo. Theo grabbed Miguel with both hands on his jacket and lifted him off the ground with very little effort. "I said I don't want to go."

Antonio quickly stuck his gun into Theo's face. "Put him down or I'm going to kill you right here in the street."

Theo dropped Miguel and smiled as the smaller man tripped over himself. "Won't your friend be upset if you kill me?" Theo said joking.

"Then Señor, our friend will have to learn to live with the disappointment. Please get into the car." As Theo entered the car, Antonio swung his fist and slammed Theo in the back of his head, and watched as Theo he fell sideways onto the seat.

* * * * *

When Theo awoke, he was tied to a chair. He shook his head to clear it. The room was dimly lit, but he could see them sitting at a table playing cards. "Hey, you," Theo yelled out, "you better damn well let me loose."

"In time we will untie you. We do not wish to fight with you. So it is best you stay that way," Miguel responded.

Theo struggled against the ropes. He was angry now. "When I get loose I am going to choke the life out of the both of you!"

Antonio snapped on a pair of leather gloves and walked over to Theo. "Señor you are making too much noise; you give me a headache." He swung at Theo, slicing a gash above his left eyebrow. A trickle of warm blood flowed down the side of his face.

"I'm going to rip your head off," Theo groaned.

"I am sorry, Señor, but you forced me to do it."

* * * * *

About an hour later, Theo heard the elevator motor start. His head was still foggy from the blow Antonio had given him, and he struggled to stay alert. Theo watched as Antonio walked over to the elevator door and raised it. "Señorita, we have done as you asked. We have brought the big man here," he said to someone still hidden inside the depths of the elevator.

"Where is he?" She could not see him in the shadows. Miguel turned on the lights, and Frankie saw Theo tied to the chair, dried blood caked on his face. "Why the hell have you got him tied up?" she cried, and walked over to her old friend.

"I am sorry, Señorita, but he was most difficult. We could not help it." Frankie saw the blood dripping from the gash over Theo's eyebrow. Then she turned to Antonio. "I told you not to hurt him, didn't I?" she screamed, and slapped Antonio's face.

He stepped back and put a hand inside his jacket. "Go ahead and try it," she challenged.

Miguel got between them. "Do not be foolish, amigo. Señor Montoya would not like this." Antonio took a deep breath, turned and walked away.

"Little lady, it looks like you found me before I could find you," Theo said weakly.

"I am sorry about this Theo; all I wanted was to talk to you."

"Cut me loose, little lady, so I can hurt them real bad."

Frankie found a first aid box on top of the refrigerator and knelt with it before Theo. "First thing's first," she said, pouring peroxide on a cotton swab and laying it against the cut. "This is going to hurt you just a little."

Theo winced as the peroxide soaked into the wound and Frankie bandaged the gash. "I'm going to send them away for now. Then I am going to cut you loose and we are going to talk."

Frankie walked over to Miguel and Antonio and spoke to them, but Theo could not hear what they were saying. Both men disappeared into the elevator and were gone in a few seconds. Frankie turned to Theo. "I want you to know that this

was not meant to happen. All I wanted was to talk to you. And
as far as they are concerned, they only did what they thought
was right, okay?"

"I believe you would not hurt me intentionally," Theo said
sincerely.

Frankie cut Theo loose. "Come on. I'll buy you a beer."
They walked over to the card table. Frankie took four bottles
out of the refrigerator and handed Theo two, then sat down.
"After I explain some things you'll understand why things
happened this way. And after I tell you what I know, if you do
not believe me, you can take me back to Doc, no tricks. Is that
fair enough?"

"Yes, I think that's fair," Theo said.

"And you bite the bullet with these guys, no getting even."

"Okay, I promise," Theo said, sounding like a kid.

Frankie took a sip of her beer. "How much do you know
about the diamond robbery?" she asked.

"Not much except the people who were in it. Doc kept
everything on the quiet side. He told me the reason he wouldn't
say anything to me was because it was best that I didn't know."

Frankie laughed.

"I don't see what's so funny," Theo said looking insulted.

"My God, Theodore. You are either very trusting or very
stupid."

"I don't like that kind of talk, little lady. And I said to
never call me Theodore."

"Okay, I'm sorry. Didn't it ever dawn on you that four
people pulled off that job and they're all dead?

"Doc said they were accidents."

"Accidents, accidents," Frankie repeated. "Louis, who had
been taking care of his pigeons on that roof since he was
fourteen, accidentally falls off his roof. Give me a break, Theo.
And a car runs over Murray in Harlem, no less. And not only

that, it runs over him three times --- Murray, who was afraid of his own shadow. He wouldn't even throw the trash out after dark if he were alone. What was he doing in Harlem? You still think these were accidents?"

"Why would Doc do that?"

"Let me finish. Jay was in a shootout in an alley. Jason never carried a gun in his life. Damn it, Theo he was afraid of the stupid things. Theo, even you knew that. And Eddie was killed five minutes before he was to meet me. He died in my arms. And what about me?"

Theo listened, not wanting to believe what he was hearing. "I know you have no reason to lie to me, but neither does Doc."

"Theo, I could have had you killed instead of having you brought here to talk. I could have made them force you to tell them where Doc is."

"I have to think about all this; it's too much for me at one time," Theo said, sounding confused.

"Did you know that there was a hundred million in diamonds stolen and not sixty like he told you there was?" Frankie continued. "Did Doc tell you that there were twenty kilos of heroin in the safe with the diamonds? Or did it slip his mind?"

Theo looked at her in disbelief. Frankie knew that Theo was finding it hard to come to the reality of the situation. He started to say something, but instead just shook his head in disbelief.

"And try this on for size," she said. "Why did Doc go through so much trouble to cover up the fact that he's alive? And if you were going with him, why has he not done the same for you? Where is your passport, where are your plane tickets? The car is rented under your name, so is your parking spot and apartment. Why haven't the cops come looking for you?

Because after you deliver me to him, you're going to have an accident, and so am I."

"A lot of things seem clear to me now, little lady, but I still don't understand why he would want to hurt anybody,"

"Theo, greed is a terrible thing. It can turn ordinary people into monsters."

"What do you want me to do? Knowing all this, I can't take you to Doc."

"I know that you transferred your money to the Bahamas International Bank. And I know you are packed and you were ready to leave after you deliver me. Knowing this, if I were lying, you would be dead now. I will help you to get to the Bahamas safely if you tell me where Doc is."

Theo took the last sip from his bottle. "Little lady, I knew you were smart, and if anybody can outsmart Doc, it's going to be you."

"Thanks for that vote of confidence. So now tell me where he is."

"I can't do that. I owe Doc too much."

"No, Theo. He planned to kill you when you brought me back."

Theo looked drawn and Frankie knew that his loyalty to Doc was unshakeable. "I won't tell you little lady. I still owe him something."

"Okay," Frankie said. "I understand how you feel. I'll find him anyway. When he realizes you're gone, he'll send someone else to find me, and I'll be ready for them."

"I don't want to go against Doc, but I don't want to see you hurt. Maybe I should stay here."

"No, I think things may get too complicated if you stay. Besides, I still have Miguel and Antonio if I need them."

"Them," Theo said with contempt. "I could crush both of them with one hand."

"I know you could. But you promised not to try and get even."

"I'll do as you ask."

"They will be back in a while. Your bags and assets are packed and ready for you when it's time to go."

Theo looked surprised. "You seem to have everything figured out."

"By now your car has disappeared, and there is no record of a parking place in your name, and your apartment is emptied of anything that could tell where you are going. Someone will drive you to New Jersey and you will take a flight to Miami. Midge will meet you and make sure you get to where you're going."

The motor engaged as the elevator started up and came to a stop. The door lifted and three men stepped into the loft. Antonio approached Frankie. "This is Señor Ortega. He will take Señor Theo to the airport. We are ready to go."

"Goodbye, little lady. Come visit me when you can," Theo said as he got in the elevator.

"I will, Theo." Frankie said, watching Theo as the elevator descended. She thought it best not to tell him that Antonio found a map of Vermont.

* * * * *

Events surrounding her return from prison had moved in such a manner that Frankie did not have time to think of her parents. Now she wondered if fate had brought her to Delancey Street, where her father had his clothing store. A sign on the doors said "Closed" in bright red letters. She could never remember a day, except for Saturdays, that her father kept the shop closed. In her mind, she could hear his words spoken to her mother: "Sophia, come rain or shine, the store must stay open."

A familiar voice startled her. "Francine, I didn't know you were back home; how is your father doing?"

Frankie turned to see Mr. Gould standing next to her "I don't know. I just returned. Why is the store closed?" she asked.

"You know, Aaron never closes the store, no matter what. So I called your house." Frankie wished he would get to the point. "Your mother answered and she was crying."

Frankie was growing impatient. "Mr. Gould, please, what happened?"

"She said your father had a heart attack."

"Is he dead?" Frankie asked

"I don't know. Your momma said he was in intensive care; that is all I know."

"Do you know where he is?" Frankie asked, nearly pleading.

"I think he is in Doctor's Hospital," he said.

Frankie then hailed a cab before Mr. Gould could finish speaking.

"Doctor's Hospital, quickly," she ordered the driver and slammed the door shut.

"It was nice talking to you again," Mister Gould yelled out as the cab pulled away.

* * * * *

Frankie spotted her mother as she entered the waiting room. Her mother saw her and the two women embraced. "How is he doing?" Frankie asked.

"They said he was resting. He has a fifty-fifty chance. This was the worst." Frankie looked at her mother in disbelief.

"What do you mean this one?"

"Your father had two last year."

"Why didn't you tell me?"

Her mother looked at her sadly. "He didn't want you to know."

"My God, Mom, do both of you hate me that much?"

Her mother started to cry, then gently put her arms around Frankie. "I could never hate you. You're my daughter. I will always love you. Please, Fran, never think that."

"Mom, he closed his heart to me. I spent six years in prison to keep Jay safe and you knew it, and you never said a word about it. What happened was not my fault."

"I know Fran, I know."

"Then why didn't you at least tell him after Jason died?"

"Fran, I swear to you I did tell him, but he would not believe me. He hit me several times. He would not speak to me for days."

"That son of a bitch!" Frankie growled.

Her mother grabbed her by the shoulders and shook her angrily. "Don't say that. He is your father. That man in there is my life. Do you understand? Never say that again. Never!"

Frankie could no longer hold the tears back. Hugging her mother, she said," I'm sorry, Mom. I am sorry."

Sophia wiped her tears with a tissue. "Fran, your sister will be here soon, so please --- no fighting."

"That's up to her, Mom. You know I'm not good at turning the other cheek," she said, trying to smile. Their conversation turned into small talk as they settled down to wait. A little while later, a doctor wearing a white coat came out to speak with them. "He's resting now. We'll know more in a few hours," he said.

* * * * *

Laura and her husband stepped off the elevator and walked to the waiting area. "Momma," she cried out and ran to Sophia. "How is Dad doing?"

Sophia stood up to embrace her other daughter. Fresh tears started in her eyes. "He's resting now. The doctor said he has a good chance. All we can do is pray."

Laura spotted Frankie and sneered. "Well, look who's here --- the jail bird. What did you do, break out of prison?"

Frankie smiled slyly. "You still giving head for twenty dollars a pop?" Frankie laughed.

"Momma, tell her she shouldn't talk to me that way," Laura pleaded with Sophia.

Laura's husband stepped between the two women and faced Frankie. "You can't talk to my wife like that."

"Well, if it isn't baby Lenny."

Sophia came between them. "Stop it, you two!" she said sharply. "Your father is in there, on his deathbed and you're acting like children. Now stop it!"

"But, Mom, it's her fault daddy is in there," Laura charged.

"Mom, she says one more thing and I'm going to deck her and her husband if he gets in the way!"

Sophia's face reddened. She grabbed each daughter by the arm and shook them. "I warn you both. I will not tolerate this bickering. Now shut up both of you and sit down!"

* * * * *

The morning found the small group sleeping in the waiting room. Sophie was the first to awaken. She rubbed her eyes and noticed that the doctor was walking towards them. Sophia stood up. "Ira how is he?" she asked, her voice pleading for good news.

"He's doing fine, Sophie. He made it this time. You're

going to have to get him to slow down, or next time he may not be so lucky."

"This time I will take charge. I'll make him slow down. Can we see him now?"

"No, I don't want him disturbed today," Ira said sternly. "All of you go home and come back tomorrow. He needs the rest."

Sophia then woke Laura and Frankie and relayed the message.

Laura ignored her sister. "I will see you tomorrow, Mom," she said with a huff and walked away.

"Well, Mom, see you around. Here's my number if you need me. I'll be there for a week or two," Frankie said. She kissed her mother on the cheek.

"Fran, aren't you coming back to see your father tomorrow?"

"No, Mom. You want him to have another heart attack? Maybe when he learns not to hate so much. Maybe then. Actually, I would rather that you didn't mention that I was here."

Frankie turned in an effort to hide her emotions from her mother, and walked away. She had learned to do that well. Frankie was relieved to know her father would be all right. She had resigned herself to the fact that her father was an unforgiving man. But her mother knew the truth, and in her heart Sophia knew there was nothing to be forgiven for because Frankie had done nothing wrong.

CHAPTER SIX

AN EYE FOR AN EYE

Frankie was not a religious person, but she felt that if she talked to Rabbi Newberg, he might be able to help her. Her father and the Rabbi had been boyhood friends in Poland and had come to America together. Knowing her father and mother so well, she thought he could help. Frankie told him her story from beginning to end, leaving out what she felt he had no need to know. After a stiff lecture, he told her what amounted to "turn the other cheek."

* * * * *

Frankie sat alone in her apartment. She would have to make a decision about what she should do. Should she turn the other cheek and leave retribution to God, or should she proceed as she had all her life? She had heard the words "retribution" and "don't worry; God will punish them," and she had seen so much evil flourish, she thought that if God were there, why was he ignoring these people? Turning the other cheek never kept anyone from taking your school lunch money, or anyone from hurting you. No, these were the words of people who where afraid to fight back. Even if this retribution thing did work, it just took too damned long. And she could not wait for a lifetime to go by. If God did punish Doc for what he did, Frankie decided she wanted to be the one to help Doc get to his judgment day a little quicker. An eye for an eye was fair in her book.

There wasn't much to do but wait. Frankie knew that as

soon as Doc realized Theo had deserted him, he would find someone else to send after her. It was just a matter of time. She would be wasting her time if she tried to find him. The map Antonio and Miguel had found in Theo's car had given her a clue as to where Doc was hiding --- somewhere in New England or possibly Vermont. Frankie was about to leave when the phone rang. Picking up the receiver she said, "Frankie here, Mom what's wrong? You want to see me? Why?"

"Lunch sounds good. Where?" they agreed on a place to eat. After Frankie hung up she stood staring at the phone. *That was very odd, my mother calling me to have lunch with her,* she thought. "Wonders never cease," she said out loud to herself and headed out of the apartment.

Twenty minutes later, she met her mother at Katz's Deli. They had decided to have a late lunch to miss the corporate crowd. Halfway through her pastrami sandwich, Sophia opened up to Frankie. "Fran, I must ask you a favor," she said, sounding unsure of her self. "I...I don't know how to say this."

"Mom, just say it," Frankie sighed.

"This is most difficult to ask, because of our past relationship." Sofia sounded embarrassed.

"You mean you want me out of town before noon," Frankie joked.

"Goodness no, Fran. I would never say that to you."

"Relax, Mom, it's just a joke."

"Oh, I see," Sofia said, relieved."

"Will you please tell me what you want?"

"Your father will not be able to work for at least a year, not even leave the house, except to sit in the yard. It will be a most difficult year for him."

"What does that have to with me?"

"Fran, I want you to help me run the business until your father is well again."

Frankie was incredulous. "You're joking. Are you out of your mind? You want me to help the very man who hates my guts?" Frankie laughed. "You must have lost your mind."

"Fran, you're the only one I can depend on."

"What about your daughter, sweet Laura?" Frankie huffed.

"Fran, she is not capable. She has no, what is it you always use to call her -- a des?" Sofie said, unsure of the word.

"No, Momma. Dufus --- someone who can't do anything right."

Her mother interrupted. "I get the idea and I am ashamed to say my daughter is a dufus." The women looked at each other, and Sofia burst out laughing.

"Mom, you're too much."

"Fran, will you please help me?"

"Mom, both of you have enough money to sell the store and retire."

"Yes, Fran, I know, and we will, as soon as I can convince your father it's his idea," she said slyly, then added "meanwhile, I need your help."

Frankie thought for a moment. "On one condition, and that is that you not tell him I am helping you, and no interference from your favorite daughter."

"Yes, you can have whatever you want."

Frankie was reluctant to say yes, but her mother needed her. *Well*, she thought, *I need something to do while I'm waiting for Doc to find me.* "There is one thing I have to warn you about, Momma."

"What is that, Fran?"

"If you try fixing me up with any dates, I'm out of here."

"But, Fran there are some nice eligible bachelors."

"Mom, I warn you --- don't even think about it."

"I understand, Fran. I'll try to remember that."

* * * * *

Monday proved to be a busy day, and. dickering for price had come easy to Frankie. As a young girl she had watched her grandfather, then her father, haggling for the price of an item. She had learned from her grandfather that dickering, or haggling, as the Americans called it, was the way business was done in the old country. It was a tradition. It was good for business because both parties always came to an agreement. And both parties came away from the haggling process feeling like they were the winner.

Frankie enjoyed working with her mother, getting to know her and realizing that her mother was a much more independent and intelligent woman than she had pretended to be.

The week went quite fast and on Friday they closed early in preparation for Saturday.

"Fran, will you come to temple with us tomorrow?"

"No, Momma. Do you want the walls to fall down?" Frankie joked.

"Fran, you must not talk like that. It's not nice."

"Besides, Papa will be there, and I don't want to cause any trouble." Frankie was looking forward to a weekend of relaxing. She missed Midge. Besides Midge, Frankie had no close friends. For the most part, she had always been a loner. There had been some men in her life, but nothing serious. Frankie wondered how her mother stayed married to her father all these years; she would have to ask her someday. Meanwhile, Frankie decided to go home and soak in a hot tub to relax.

* * * * *

Doc sat on his front porch enjoying the summer breeze. He glanced at his wrist and checked the time and watched the car as it turned onto the driveway. The thick, lush greenery hid the driveway from the road. He knew it would be Harry Sims. Doc had called Harry two days before. If anybody could find Frankie and Theo, he was the man to do it. There was a second man with him. Doc was curious about that, because Harry always worked alone, but as long as this job got done, what was the difference? The car slowed to a stop as it reached the porch.

Doc stood up to greet the two men as they exited the car and walked up the porch steps. They shook hands.

"It's been a long time, Doc," Harry said.

"Harry, it's good to see you," Doc replied, eyeing the younger man.

"Doc this is Dave, my brother Al's son. He wants me to break him into the business."

"Harry, I can't afford any mistakes," Doc said, handing him a white envelope.

"Don't worry, Doc, have I ever let you down?" Harry asked confidently.

"Just be sure you keep it that way," Doc said, his eyes flashing. "Find out what happened to Theo. If he's not already dead, find Frankie and Midge, make them all disappear forever!"

Doc handed Harry a folder. "Everything you need to know about them is in here."

"You worry too much, Doc. How much trouble can one woman be? Don't worry."

"You never ran into anyone like Frankie; she's a sly bitch. And I won't be happy until she's in her grave," Doc said.

"Give me two weeks and all your troubles will be over," Harry said as they walked to the door.

* * * * *

The second week working at the store was less hectic, and the awkwardness of working with her mother had lessened. Frankie was actually beginning to enjoy it. She wondered when her sister would show up and cause more trouble. Frankie knew Doc would send someone to get her soon --- under normal circumstances, she would have been worried, but Ricardo Montoya, now realizing that there was still a chance to get his diamonds and drugs back, had made it clear to her that he had someone watching her at all times --- they were never far away. Everyday they followed her to and from work.

* * * * *

"Frannie, come and have some tea," her mother called out. Frankie walked through the curtains that separated the store from the stock room and fitting area in the back. Sophia handed her daughter a cup of tea. Spread out on the small table were two bagels. "Here, take one --- cream cheese and lox," Sophia said cheerfully, handing one to Frankie. "Come and eat. We have a long morning ahead of us."

"You know, Mom, you're going to spoil me," she kidded.

"Your father always says a good breakfast is important when you have to do a day's work."

"How is Papa doing?" Frankie asked.

"Better every day," her mother replied, stirring sugar into her teacup.

"Momma, there is something I would like you to do for me, if you wouldn't mind."

"What is it, dear?" Her mother asked warmly.

"Well, I am a bit uncomfortable being called Fran. Could you please call me Frankie like my friends do?" she asked.

"But, Fran, I am your mother, not your friend."

"But we should be friends, too."

Her mother thought for a minute, and taking the last sip of her tea said, "So, okay. From now on you are Frankie. Okay, Fran?" Sophia smiled.

"Frankie I made my first joke. Not a good one, but a joke. What do you think, Frankie?"

"You'll get there yet, Momma."

* * * * *

The day Frankie had dreaded had come. Her mother was in the back room doing alterations on some of the garments that had been sold, when Frankie looked up and saw her sister coming into the store with her husband behind her. Laura spotted Frankie and spoke without looking at her sister. "Where is my mother?" she asked curtly.

Frankie pointed to the back wordlessly. Laura brushed past Frankie, her husband following close behind like a puppy on her heels. Frankie stuck her foot out slightly as Lenny passed; tripping him and making him bump into his wife.

"Damn it, Lenny! Can't you be more careful?" she snapped.

Frankie winked at Lenny as he looked back at her. They disappeared behind the curtains, but Frankie could hear them talking. Laura was complaining about Frankie's working in the store.

Frankie had promised not to fight with Laura, but when her sister suggested to their mother that Frankie would dip her fingers into the till and steal the day's receipts, that was all she could take. Frankie went into the back room and smiled angelically. "Momma, would you take Lenny to Grossman's to look at the pressing machine and see if we are getting a good price? I want to talk to my sister for a few minutes."

Sophia was reluctant to leave, but she took Lenny by the arm, almost dragging him outside. "Yes, it is a good thing you have come. Let's go look at the pressing machine."

Frankie waited until the door closed. "I promised Momma that I would not fight with you, but when you accuse me of being a thief and stealing from my own family, I have to draw the line."

"Well, I wasn't the one who went to jail," Laura sniffed.

"You're not making it easy for me to be friends with you," Frankie said.

"Drop dead, jailbird."

Frankie stepped back and hit Laura across the cheek with the back of her hand as hard as she could.

Laura backed up and started to cry. "You hit me! I'm going to tell Momma on you!"

"Hit you?" Frankie sneered. "No, that was just a love tap to get your attention. That wasn't hitting. This is hitting!" Frankie drew back her arm and sank a punch into Laura's left jaw. Laura stumbled backwards and fell over a box. Frankie kneeled down beside her. "Now I want you to listen to me, big sister. I don't give a rat's ass if you like me or not, but if you don't watch your manners, I'm going to rip your tongue out. Do you understand?"

"Don't worry. I'm not going to hit you again," Frankie said, hauling her sister up from the floor and helping her into a chair. Laura rubbed her jaw.

"Laurie, you're a spoiled brat who never did anything for anyone unless you got something out of it."

"That's not true. You were always jealous of me," Laura pouted.

"I want you to listen to me. Do you know why I went to jail?"

"Because you stole something."

Frankie laughed. "You really don't know, do you? Well, let me give you some facts, my dear sister. I took the rap for your brother so he would not go to jail. Ask Momma. She'll tell you I'm not lying."

"Poppa says you're a liar and a thief and I don't believe anything you say about my brother."

"Then just stay out of my way, you understand?"

Laura touched her face again. "Ouch! You really hurt me, Frannie." She walked over to the door-length mirror. "My God, you bastard. You gave me a black eye. And I've got a PTA meeting tonight,"

"Stop your whining. A little make-up and you'll be all right," Frankie suggested. "This is a good time for you to give back some of what you've taken all these years. It doesn't matter what you think of me. I make no excuses for my life, and I don't ask for absolution for my sins, but at least I don't pretend to be what I am not."

"You know, Frannie, the truth of the matter is that I've always been jealous of you. I used to wish I could be like you, even though I was older than you. Poppa always depended on you to for everything. But after the way you turned out, I'm glad I'm not you."

"Fran, Mom would say anything to protect you from the truth, and I wouldn't believe you if you swore on a stack of bibles."

The door to the shop opened and their mother came in with Lenny behind her. He looked at his wife. "Laurie, honey. Look at your eye," he cried, and hurried to her side. He tilted her head up to the light. "What happened? She didn't hurt you, did she?"

Sophie went to Laura and looked at the eye, then glanced at Frankie, who looked up at the ceiling.

Laurie pushed her husband away. "It's no big deal. I was helping Fran move some stock, and walked into the door. There isn't very much room back there."

Both Lenny and Sophia knew she was lying, but decided it was best not to say any more about it. Frankie looked at her sister in a different light, as though maybe her big sister was finally growing up.

* * * * *

Midge had found a villa in Coral Gables with a great view of the ocean. She sat by the pool reading a letter she had received from Karen. She was happy to know that things were going well for her friend. The letters said that the doctors had been able remove almost ninety percent of her scars and minimize the rest, that if she did not hear from her for a while not to worry --- they were going to start on her face next. The doctors, Karen wrote, said the surgery would be complicated, but they would do the very best they could. She added a postscript, saying how much she would love for Midge and Frankie to be there when the bandages came off. Midge started to write a letter back, letting Karen know they would do their best to be there. Midway through, Midge set her pen down and took another sip of her drink. She wanted to call Frankie and let her know what was going on. She thought about Otto. He had taken her out several times, but had never tried anything with her. He always treated her like a lady. She remembered asking him why he never tried anything and his answer was that he was in love with her and didn't want her for a one-night stand. Midge smiled, thinking that she had decided to take a chance on him, something she had never regretted. He was a good man and if he weren't so greedy, he would still be here now. Perhaps it was time to find a steady guy.

* * * * *

Harry Sims had never liked New York City. He had always considered it too unpredictable a place; there were just too damn many people. He did not like the fact that Frankie was so easy to find; she was living out in the open, not trying to hide. It was as if she were waiting for someone to come for her. Doc's words echoed in his ears: *"Be careful. She is a sly bitch. Don't take her for granted."*

He told Doc with confidence that he always gets what he goes after. Harry thought Frankie was a good-looking babe, but he didn't see anything special about her. This would be easy. Harry then contacted Doc to let him know he had located Frankie, and that Theo had seemingly disappeared from the face of the earth. So now Harry settled down to wait for his chance. He put his nephew on guard duty, watching the store while he watched Frankie's apartment. Harry watched Frankie as she exited the building. He noticed that she was a creature of habit, never deviating from her schedule. She never had company, nor did she appear to date. When she did go out, she went alone and never stayed out late. It wasn't until the fifth day that he realized that not only was *he* following her, but someone else was following her, too.

At a red light, he called Dave's cell phone number to tell him not to waste any time and get to the safe house quickly, making sure he wasn't being tailed. Harry watched Frankie get on a bus, and as it pulled away, he put the car in gear. He tagged the bus for a couple of blocks along its route then made a left turn. Harry drove around for an hour until he was satisfied he wasn't being followed then headed for the Holland tunnel into New Jersey.

* * * * *

Harry walked into the old two-story house and was greeted by his nephew. "What went wrong, Uncle Harry?" Dave asked impatiently.

Harry took off his jacket and removed his shoulder holster. "What went wrong? Well for one thing, while we were watching her, someone else was watching her."

"You got to be kidding. How could that be?"

"I don't know, except that there must be more to this than Doc was willing to tell us."

"Maybe we should forget about the whole thing, Uncle Harry."

"Do me a favor, kid. I asked you before --- stop calling me uncle."

"What do you want to do, Harry?" Harry didn't answer. He dialed a number on his cell phone and paced the floor waiting for an answer. Finally he heard the graveled voice. "Yeah? Who's calling?" Doc challenged.

"It's me. Harry," he answered.

"Damn, you got her already?"

"No, but..."

Doc interrupted before Harry could finish talking.

"Then why the hell are you bothering me?"

"Shut up and listen to me. What kind of a con are you pulling on me?"

Doc was flustered for a moment. "I don't understand Harry. What's wrong?"

"For one thing, while I was watching her movements, someone else was watching her, too. And it wasn't the cops."

"I told you she was a sly one," Doc said dryly.

"Save it for someone who doesn't know you. If I continue, the price goes up. Otherwise, get someone else to do the job."

Doc was quiet for a few seconds. Harry could hear his heavy breathing. "Well --- make up your mind, I've got other things to do."

"How much more do you want?"

Harry smiled. "Thirty five."

"Thirty five!" Doc yelled.

"Take it or leave it," Harry said with finality.

"All right, go on and I'll send you the money!"

"It's going to take a bit longer, but you will get your delivery," Harry said, hanging up on Doc.

"What do we do now?" Dave asked.

"I don't know yet. I have to think about it a while."

"Harry, I am a bit confused. Were we being watched, or not?" Dave asked.

"I don't know yet." Harry repeated, plopping down on the sofa.

He was quiet for a while, then said, "I don't think they were watching her. It was more likely they were looking out for her. She must have hired some muscle. Doc was right about her --- she is one slick lady."

"The first thing to do is find out who they are... I knew this was too easy; she's been waiting for us to come.

"When do we start?" David asked.

"We don't start. You take a few days off and relax. This is a one-man job. Don't worry; you'll get your chance."

Dave looked upset about being left out of things. "You sure there's nothing I can do?" David asked again.

"Yes, there is. Don't shave for the next few days."

Dave shrugged his shoulders. "If that's what you want."

"Come on. We'll go out and eat. There's a Chinese restaurant not far from here."

* * * * *

The next morning, Harry exchanged his rental car for

another one, and parked it several blocks away from Frankie's apartment house. Harry hated this city and its alternate side of the street parking days. He was a little early, and only a few of the shops were open, so managing to get to the roof of one of the stores was fairly easy. The buildings were all joined together, so it was just a matter of climbing over a two-foot wall to get from one building to another. From the roof of the third store he had a clear view of the shop where Frankie worked. The skies were a grayish blue. He hoped it wouldn't rain, but he had a cheep plastic raincoat with him today, just in case. Harry picked a spot and settled down to wait.

* * * * *

It rained on and off all day, but Harry's determination kept him on the roof. At forty-seven, Harry felt tired and run down, but attributed that to the decadent lifestyle he lived. He ate and drank well and lived life in the fast lane sometimes, but he enjoyed it, so what the hell. But he decided to retire soon, which was why he had taken David under his wing. Whichever way things turned out, this would be his last job, and it would be time for Dave to go it on his own. Harry wanted to spend more time with his wife, maybe take a trip.

He watched as Frankie walked to the bus stop. He noticed that her bodyguards didn't follow her home, but drove ahead of her and disappeared in traffic. Tomorrow he would come back again, and this time he would get there just before she left the store, park and wait for them to leave. Then he would follow them.

* * * * *

Harry opened the door to the house and the smell of pizza

hit him as he stepped into the foyer. "That smells good," he said, taking off his windbreaker and shoulder holster.

"Want a beer, Harry?" David called out.

"Yeah, I think so. It's been a rough day," Harry said tiredly.

Both men ate, sharing some small talk, until Dave's curiosity got the best of him.

"Harry, I hate to be a pain in the butt, but I'm dying here, so you have to tell me what's going on."

"Well, I found out that they watch every move she makes during the day. But they don't follow her home. Tomorrow I'll follow them and find out where they go. The day after that, I'll find out if anyone's watching the house. Then we can make our plans. We may have to snatch her on the bus ride home or at her apartment. We'll know more in a few days."

"I feel better now that I know something. By the way, can I shave now?" Dave asked hopefully.

"No, Davie, not yet."

"What does that mean, Harry?"

"Well, because if things go right, I'm going to let you solo."

"You're going to let me nab her alone?" Dave asked incredulously. Harry nodded.

"You're kidding. You mean I'm finally on my own?" Dave said, sounding to Harry like an eager child who had just found a shiny new bicycle under the Christmas tree.

"Not quite. I'll be there, just as an observer, or in case something goes wrong. If not, the next job is yours," Harry said, laughing. He looked at his nephew then shook his head. "You shouldn't take life so seriously, Davie." He pushed back his chair and stood up. "Good night, kid. I'm worn out, I need some sleep. "

* * * * *

Harry parked the car on a side street a few blocks from the shop the next morning and left it there. Then he went to a movie, timing everything so he would be back before Frankie got on the bus.

* * * * *

He was in his car when they pulled out, and he followed them. The car got to Frankie's apartment five minutes before the bus arrived. One of the men got out and disappeared into the doorway of the next building. Then the car pulled away.

The car he was following pulled up in front the Spanish embassy. Two men got out and the car pulled away. There was no need for Harry to go any further. He found out all he wanted to know, and he didn't like it one bit.

* * * * *

Harry called Doc first thing in the morning with the information he now had. He asked Doc why the Spanish embassy would be watching Frankie. He wanted to know more about what was going on. Even Doc's offer of more money could not persuade him. He told Doc that he would send half the money back to him because he had been lied to. Harry could pretty much figure out what was going on, and what was going on probably had to do with drugs. These people had a long reach and he wanted no part of it, but as far as he was concerned, Doc could do whatever he wanted with the information. He was out of it. Harry knew one thing for sure -- - he wanted to stay alive long enough to enjoy his retirement.

* * * * *

Doc hung up and pounded his fist on the desk. "Damn!" He was angrier at himself than with Harry. Montoya, it had to be him, it couldn't be the cops; they would have picked Frankie up already. No, it had to be Montoya, and if it was, he would know all about Doc if Frankie had found out he was alive. Doc cursed himself again for playing games and not killing Frankie himself. He wouldn't be in this mess if he'd just gotten rid of Frankie. Now he'll have to find someone else to kill her. This was getting complicated and he didn't like it. Meanwhile, he would start making arrangements to leave the country. Doc kept almost everything packed and stored in the attic until he needed it. The money was in a Swiss bank account and the diamonds were hidden away. He complemented himself on the brilliant way he had hidden the heroin. *In plain sight.* He thought,

Frankie seemed to live a charmed life, so he would continue to worry until she was in her grave. To hell with Harry if he didn't finish the job. He knew people who would do it, and for less money.

Doc cursed himself again. He should have given her both Jay's share and her share. It would have been an easy price to pay, but being angry with himself wasn't going to change things now. He had planned for years, waiting for just the right time and the right job to come along. Doc had lived and breathed for this daily, and he was dammed if he was going to let Frankie spoil things for him now.

* * * * *

Doc spent the rest of the day repacking what little he had unpacked, and dumped his bags in the living room. He had a bust of the Roman Emperor Caesar crated up. As soon as Frankie was out of the way, he would take it to the airport and send it through customs using his new identity, where he had paid to have someone pass the statue and his luggage through without any trouble. Then he would be on his way to a life of luxury for the rest of his life. And the irony of it all was that Doc would sell Ricardo Montoya's drugs back to him. It made Doc happy to know that Montoya would pay twice for the same thing. It would be easy to find someone else to get rid of Frankie. There were a lot of mugs out there who wanted to make a name for themselves.

If the next person he sent for Frankie failed, he swore he would go back and do it himself, no matter what the cost. He glanced at his watch --- it was time for his appointment with the realty company. He had managed to rid himself of two of the businesses he owned. The house and property were next to be sold. He had to go into town to meet with a potential buyer. He put on his jacket and headed out back to the garage to get his car, humming as he walked. Making money always made him happy.

* * * * *

It was a slow day at the store, and Frankie was getting restless. When the phone rang in the back room and her mother called out that it was for her, she sighed with relief. She was not used to being cooped up in one place. The days her sister came to help out weren't so bad because she could leave the store a little early. "Who is it, Mom?" she yelled out.

"It's your friend, Midge." Sophie scowled with disapproval and handed Frankie the phone.

Frankie put her hand over the mouthpiece and stuck her tongue out at her playfully. "Momma, you're such a prude."

Sophie grinned. "I'll just leave you alone with your *friend frau der nacht,"* Sophie sniffed, showing her dislike for Midge.

"I see your mother still doesn't like me," Midge began.

"You heard that. I'm sorry, Midge."

"Don't let it bother you. Listen, I got a beautiful villa for us. How is everything going?"

Frankie gave Midge a rundown on everything that had happened.

"Frankie, it's getting lonely down here, so come on down for a few days. We can have a real ball," Midge said excitedly.

"I don't know if I can get away."

"Come on," Midge pleaded. "You waited this long for Doc to make a move. You can wait a few more days. Come on. Pretty please? Besides, you need some relaxation."

Frankie thought it over. "I don't know, Midge. It may be a bad idea."

"Frankie, if you're not there when he comes, he'll wait. It will frustrate him more. Besides, if your plan doesn't work and you wind up dead, look at what you're going to miss."

"You may be right, Midge. I'll come down."

"You sure you're coming?"

"Yes, I said I was. I'll call you Monday morning and let you know what time I'll arrive."

"Yes!" Midge yelled. "I know exactly what you need. I got a nice Cuban stud that'll kick your hormones into gear. I'll see you," she said, and hung up before Frankie could answer.

Sophie entered the back room as Frankie laid the phone in the cradle. "Are you finished with your friend? I suppose you will be leaving soon," her mother said sadly.

"Momma, I know what you think of Midge, but remember this... when everyone turned their back on me, and I had no where to live, she was there for me. She was the only friend I had, so, please --- from now on I don't want to hear anything bad about her." Sophie looked at her daughter sympathetically. "Fran, I am sorry. It is hard for me to admit, but you are right. We did treat you very badly. I guess there is no way to make up for how we treated you. Your friend was more understanding than your own family. So you will never hear me speak badly about Midge again.

"Thank you, Momma. I really appreciate that."

"Fran, are you sure you won't come to the house to see your father?"

"No, Momma. I told you how I feel about it and that's that."

"Frankie, please."

Frankie smiled. "Momma why don't you go? I can close up myself. It will give you a little extra time with him."

"Maybe you will come to the house next week and see him."

"You never stop trying, do you, Momma?"

"No, my dear Frankie, there are even some things that you don't know, as smart as you think you are."

"What do you mean by that, Momma?"

"I have no more to say to you about that right now."

"Momma, you're never going to change, are you?"

Sophie grinned. "No, Frankie, I probably won't."

CHAPTER SEVEN

MORE THAN SHE BARGAINED FOR

"I want you to know that I'll be leaving for a few days and that Laura will be here to help you. I have some personal things to attend to," Frankie told her mother, who looked at her quizzically, but said nothing.

* * * * *

Frankie spent an hour checking for tourist class airline tickets, then decided that if she was going, she might as well go first class to Miami. She charged the tickets to the business, then put that amount of cash in an envelope and left it in the cash register for her mother to find. She didn't need a rental car. Midge was going to pick her up. There was a lot for her to do before she left tomorrow. She wanted to get her hair done and maybe buy some new clothes. She also wanted to let her watchdogs know she would be away for a few days, mostly for sheer entertainment purposes. It would amuse her to let them know that she knew they were there. Frankie glanced at the wall clock. It was time to close shop.

* * * * *

She spent the next day getting her hair done and shopping. Afterwards, she had a light dinner and packed two small suitcases. Her flight was at eleven-fifteen, so it wouldn't be too difficult to get a cab in the morning.

* * * * *

Frankie awoke in the middle of the night to loud banging on her door. "What the hell's going on?" she yelled and jumped out of bed. The pounding continued, and Frankie pulled on her T-shirt and panties. She grabbed the .38 out of her shoulder bag and walked into the hall. "I said who it is?" she yelled from behind the front door. There was no response, except for the pounding on the door.

Frankie cocked the hammer. "Who's there, damn it?" she again shouted through the door. She held the gun in one hand took a deep breath and pulled the door open. The .38 was aimed at Antonio's face.

"Señorita, it is I, Antonio!" He yelled out and stepped back.

Frankie lowered the pistol and shook her head. "What the hell is wrong with you? You know this thing doesn't have a safety. Do you have a death wish?"

Antonio wiped his brow and looked down at Frankie. "I am sorry. I forgot how *loco* you are."

"Come in," she said impatiently, stepping aside to let Antonio through the doorway. "What's so important that you have to wake me up at three o'clock in the morning?"

"I am here to escort you to the airport."

"How the hell do you know where I'm going?"

"It is not for me to say, Señorita. We know, and that is all that you have to know," Antonio said simply.

"Why are you here this early in the morning? Do you intend to sneak up on the plane?"

"I do not understand, Señorita."

"Forget it."

"Señor Montoya would like to have breakfast with you." Antonio followed her into the kitchen.

"Face the wall," she ordered. She left the door between the kitchen and her bedroom open and started to dress. "Where is he now?" Frankie asked.

"He is downstairs in the limo waiting for you. Señor Montoya is an early riser. When you finish dressing, I will take your baggage down to the limo."

* * * * *

"Where are we going for breakfast, Señor Montoya?" Frankie asked.

"Please --- Ricardo to you," her host replied graciously. "I thought Connecticut would be nice. I have a home there also."

"But my flight leaves from JFK!"

"Do not worry, Señorita, I have taken the liberty of changing your flight to a later time. You can leave from Connecticut. There is a matter I wish to talk over with you."

"Look, I'm going to Miami for a few days to relax. I'll be back. We can talk then, or are you worried I'll run out on you?" Frankie questioned.

Ricardo laughed. "No, no, Señorita. That is not what worries me. I have a proposition for you."

Frankie interrupted. "Before you go any further, I'll call you Ricardo if you drop the Señorita, okay."

Ricardo laughed again. "If that is what you wish. Frankie, as you know, I am a very wealthy man, and I can quit this business any time I want to, and live like a king anywhere in the world for the rest of my life."

Frankie was not quite sure what this was leading up to, but she was sure she wouldn't like it. "What does that have to do with me?"

Ricardo's features indicated this was a serious matter. "This is very hard for me, so if you will be patient, I will try to say this the correct way. From the first day that I saw you, I have been quite taken with you. You are a strong woman and I would like to have you at my side. You can have anything in the world you want. I realize I am quite a bit older then you, but I can make up for that if you give me a chance."

Frankie was at a loss for words, but she could feel the anger rising in her. "You have the nerve and the audacity to think that because I was in prison that I'm some bimbo and would be your lover. You want to screw me then go back to your wife and kids at night. Then when you're finished with me you can just trade me in for a new model. No thanks, nobody uses Frankie Rose like that, and I mean nobody."

Ricardo's face reddened and they rode in silence for a while. Frankie slowly calmed down. She realized that he had done a lot for her. Frankie could have handled this better. "Look, Ricardo. I didn't mean that."

Ricardo cut her off before she could finish. "Please. I do not wish to speak of this now. You may have misunderstood my meaning."

Neither one spoke during the rest of the trip. Ricardo sat looking straight ahead. Frankie continued to look out her window, not wanting to meet his gaze.

* * * * *

The limo rolled onto the ferry at Orient Point. Frankie opened the door on her side and stepped out onto the deck. She stood by the rail looking out at the bright blue water and heard a voice behind her. "Señorita," Frankie turned and Antonio handed her a cup of black coffee. She smiled weakly and took the cup. "Thank you."

"I must say something to you," Antonio said sincerely. His dark brown eyes scanned Frankie's face. "Señor Montoya was married to a very wonderful woman and they had a daughter. They were devoted to each other. Señor Montoya was away on business when they were killed in a car crash. Both mother and daughter were killed instantly.

"That was ten years ago. You are the first woman he has shown any interest in. Señorita, you do Señor Montoya a great injustice. He was, I believe, asking you to marry him."

Frankie looked at Antonio with surprise. "*Me*? He wanted to marry *me*? Then it wasn't the money or the heroin that kept you guys hanging around watching me?"

"*Señor Montoya* did not want any harm to come to you. If that were not so, when you hit me that day at the warehouse, I would have killed you."

Frankie was shocked. "What a fool I've been. He'll probably never speak to me again. What an idiot I am."

Antonio took her cup and put his hand on her shoulder. "Señorita, we have ten minutes before we dock. Go talk to him. Explain your reason for what happened. He will listen. He is at the bow of the boat."

Ricardo's back was to Frankie as she approached him. She touched his shoulder and he turned. "Ricardo, I am truly sorry."

He tried to wave her off, and turned his back to her again. Now Frankie was angry. With both hands, she pushed him against the rail. Miguel started for her. Antonio grabbed his arm and stopped him. "Wait!" he whispered to his colleague.

"Now listen to me. I said I was sorry for acting like a jerk," Frankie yelled. Ricardo started to move to the side. "Don't move," Frankie said making a fist, "or so help me, I don't care who you are, I'll whack you one. Now you listen to me."

Ricardo leaned back on the railing and listened. Frankie lowered her voice. "I didn't know about your family. I'm sorry. You have to understand something, Ricardo. Nobody ever gave a damn about me. Except for Midge, and maybe now my mother. I lived in a dog eat dog world. I am a thief, a hustler. You name it, I've done it. The only men I have ever known only wanted one thing from me. And it's the thing I know least about. How could I know a man like you could get serious about a woman like me?"

Ricardo looked down at her wordlessly.

"Look, you can do better than me. I am not, by any stretch of the imagination, a lady, and don't pretend to be one. Well, that's all I have to say."

Ricardo put his arms on her shoulders and drew her close. She took a deep breath. Frankie knew what was going to happen, and she was confused. She didn't want this to happen. Or did she? Ricardo leaned down and kissed her gently and Frankie made no attempt to stop it. She sighed as their lips met for the second time.

Antonio's voice boomed in their ears. "Señor Montoya. We will be docking any minute."

"Take the limo to the dock. We will walk."

* * * * *

Ricardo spoke softly. "My dear Frankie, if you will now be quiet, I will speak. I am well aware of your background. That is unimportant to me. As I said before, I know we have only met on a few occasions. And I cannot explain it, but I am in love with you. So I make you this proposition. Marry me for one year, and if at the end of that time you feel that you do not or cannot love me, you may divorce me and I will give you any settlement you choose."

"Let me understand this. You're giving me a money back guarantee?"

"Frankie, I realize I am thirty two years older than you, but

I know I can make you happy if you give me the chance."

"Ricardo, all this is overwhelming. It's like Cinderella. I just don't know."

"Promise me you will think about it. Go to Miami and have a good time. Then when you come back you can give me your answer."

"Let me understand this, Ricardo. You want me to go to Miami and have a fling -- maybe find some stud and spend the night with him. You're going to let me do all this," Frankie said, more confused then before.

"Yes, I am willing to, as you say, let you have a fling. In my mind and heart I know it will be worth the chance. If I am to lose you, then it is better to know it now."

"And after I come back and I say no, what then?"

"Nothing will change as far as our deal is concerned. But that is a chance I will have to take."

* * * * *

They barely spoke over breakfast. The maid walked onto the patio carrying a phone and interrupting Frankie and Ricardo, who were each lost in their own thoughts.

"Señor Montoya, you are wanted on the phone," the maid said, and plugged the phone into a wall socket.

"Excuse me, Frankie, while I take this."

Frankie nodded and strolled over to some lounge chairs positioned under a shade tree. The maid followed. "Señorita, would you like more coffee?" she asked.

"Yes, thank you, I think I would." The maid returned with a fresh cup on a silver tray.

"Thank you. What is your name?"

"Maria, Señorita," she replied.

Frankie smiled. "That's a very pretty name. Thank you, for

the coffee, Maria."

"Thank you, Señorita, for those kind words," Maria said, as she turned to go.

Ricardo called out and walked toward Frankie, who looked up as he neared. "My dear Frankie, I must leave you for a while. I have urgent business, but I will be back before you leave, I promise."

Ricardo gently grabbed her hand, bent forward and kissed it. The kiss produced a feeling in her she could not explain. "I will leave Antonio here to take care of you," he said and smiled.

"You mean to watch me."

"No, my dear Frankie, to attend to your needs."

"You mean to watch what may become of your property," she replied without thinking.

"I would never consider one that I love property," Ricardo said as he turned to leave. Frankie blushed. She did not know why she had said that.

In a few minutes, Antonio appeared. "Señorita, would you like to see the grounds," he asked, "or would you rather just sit and relax?"

"I would like to talk, if you don't mind."

"Not if that is your wish, Señorita."

"Antonio, when I was a kid, my mother once told me that my big mouth is what always got me into trouble and that I should learn to think before I speak. And here I am at twenty three years old and I haven't learned to do it yet."

"Perhaps some day you will, Señorita."

"I hope so," she said with a shy smile. "You don't have to be so formal, by the way. Just call me Frankie."

"I have been with Señor Montoya most of my life. His bodyguard caught me breaking into his car and took me to him. When I found out whose car it was, I knew my life was over. I

130

told him that my father was dead and I needed money for food for my mother and sister. Señor Montoya sent me back to school and took care of my family. I became his bodyguard, and my sister is now a doctor. I would lay down my life for him," Antonio said proudly.

"Still, let's stop this Señorita stuff and just call me Frankie."

"To be on friendly terms with someone he loves, and who may someday be his wife, would be a good thing, but to be too familiar would be disrespectful to him. And that I would never do."

"I am sorry. I did not mean it that way, Antonio."

"I understand. And respect you for your kindness. I will be so bold as to say, Señorita, that I hope you decide to marry Señor Montoya. I believe you will be good for him."

"What I don't understand is that we have met on two occasions, and Ricardo never once made pass at me. He was always all business."

Antonio looked puzzled. "A pass. I do not understand the meaning of this word."

Frankie laughed. "Antonio, where have you been all your life? It means to force himself on me."

Antonio said. "Yes, Señorita, I know what you mean now. Regardless of the business Senior Montoya is in, he is a very reserved man, and would consider it to be in bad taste, to as you call it, make a pass at a woman, especially one he hoped to marry," Antonio said earnestly.

"What does your wife think about your job as a bodyguard?" Frankie asked.

"Señorita, I am not married as of yet."

"But you said your son would take your job?" Frankie asked.

"It is a wish of mine, Señorita. I will leave you to your

thoughts now," Antonio said, and headed toward the house.

* * * * *

Frankie lay back in her lounge chair and tried to sort everything out. She could take him up on his proposition and maybe she would learn to care for him. On the other hand, she thought, every time she had done something just for the money, she got herself into trouble. She remembered her mother and her friends talking at one of their tea parties about how there marriages were pre-arranged, and how in time they learned to care for the men they had married. But she could not remember any of them mentioning love, and that worried her. She would have to make a mental list of the good points of this arrangement and the bad points. Frankie had to admit that the first time she had met Ricardo, with his swarthy complexion and his dark hair graying at the temples, she, did feel a little turned on. She remembered thinking to herself that it must be all the olive oil in his veins that gave him that perfect tan. But now, if I had to rate his kiss, I would say, nine, maybe ten, she thought. She remembered the feel of his warm breath when he kissed her hand. That had been pretty sexy.

* * * * *

Frankie felt Maria gently nudging her awake. "Señorita, Señorita. Señor Montoya is here and is asking for you."

Frankie sat up, stretched and yawned. "Tell him I will be right there."

She put on the beautiful rose-colored dressing gown Ricardo had given her and strolled out to the patio, where he was waiting for her.

"Ricardo," she called out. "You're back so soon." She put

132

her arms around him, and stood on tiptoes to kiss him on the cheek. Then, putting her arm through his, she said, "Come and sit down. I want to talk to you." As they sat Ricardo glanced at his watch.

"Would you like to have an early dinner, *mi querida*?" he asked.

"It's only noon time."

Ricardo laughed. "No, m*i querida*, it is almost five o'clock."

Frankie looked at her watch, amazed at how fast the time had passed. "You're right! I must have dozed off without realizing it. No, if you don't mind. I am used to eating late."

"As you wish. Go on with what you were saying."

"Okay. Now I am not saying yes, but I am not saying no. You have put me in a bad situation."

"How so, Frankie?" Ricardo sounded worried.

"If my answer is going to be yes, I can't go to Miami and have a last fling. I would not feel right. It would be like cheating on you. Why that bothers me, I don't know, but it does. If I go to Miami, when I come back and say no, well, that would make me look like.... I think you know what I mean, Ricardo."

"If I am going to say no, then I should say it now. You understand?"

"*Mi querida,* I will be delighted if you say you will marry me and I will understand if you say no, but you are driving me crazy. You will. You won't. Maybe yes, maybe no. You're driving me *loco*," Ricardo repeated impatiently.

"Calm down. Now, sit and wait until I am finished. You may as well get used to it. What you see is what you get."

Ricardo clasped his hands. Then he nodded for her to finish what she was saying. "I have decided not to go to Miami. However, I would like you to cash in my tickets and fly Midge here. Then I will give you my answer."

"If that is what it takes. When would you like her to be here?"

"As soon as possible."

"Miguel," Ricardo called and Miguel stepped out from the house onto the patio to join them. "Take care of this matter at once."

Turning to Frankie, Ricardo said, "*Mi querida,* consider it done."

"Two things first," Frankie said. "Until I brush up on my Spanish, what's this *mi querida* mean and please call me Francine if I decide to say yes, okay?"

* * * * *

After a relaxing shower, Frankie plopped down on her bed and closed her eyes. *I wonder what Ricardo will think when he sees the tattoo of a red rose on my shoulder.* Frankie caught a glimpse of the moon through the curtains and walked over to the window, forgetting for a moment that she wasn't dressed. The moon was the brightest she had ever seen it. It stirred her somehow and she put on her rose colored bathrobe and padded down the hallway in bare feet toward Ricardo's room. Without knocking, she opened the door and walked in. Ricardo turned to face her and looked embarrassed that he himself was not clothed.

As she stood before him, Frankie slowly undid the ties of her robe and let it drop to the floor. The summer breeze, soft as a caress coming through the patio doors, lifted her dark hair off her shoulders. Frankie went to Ricardo and put her arms around his neck, and he pressed his warm body into hers. She pushed him back onto the edge of the bed. She took his face in her hands and their lips met. Frankie opened her warm mouth to him and let his tongue explore it. Ricardo pulled her into his arms, and they fell back onto the bed. He rolled on top of her, kissing her hungrily. Frankie moaned in ecstasy as he finally entered her, rising up to meet his body in perfect rhythm. With a final thrust, Ricardo was spent. He kissed her passionately and whispered in her ear, *"Te quiero, mi amor."*

Frankie rolled over on top of Ricardo and looked him straight in the eye. "You'd better love me, because I'm going to marry you and drive you crazy."

* * * * *

It didn't take Doc long to find two new accomplices. He knew that there was always someone around who'd do anything for the right price. Although he preferred that Harry Sims do the job, he chose two guys who came highly recommended. They were young, but supposedly very good at what they did. He had hired them under his assumed name to be on the safe side.

Doc had given them all the information they needed and promised them a bonus if they brought her to him that weekend.

* * * * *

The duo decided to grab her late at night. The fire escape stairway was positioned near the kitchen window, so getting into the house was a snap for them.

Doc knew that Tommy and Lester Mayfair were no rocket scientists, and a little unpredictable at times, but they would get the job done. He also knew that it was time to set things in motion. He had invested money in a stone quarry, plus two other businesses over the years, and until the diamond robbery he had intended to retire. Now it was time to slowly liquidate his properties so he wouldn't raise anyone's suspicion. This would have seemed strange to some people, but he remembered a guy hiding out from the mob who managed to get lost for twelve years until he made the mistake of putting an advertisement in the newspaper. He only wanted to sell his motel, but someone recognized him and sent a hit man.

It would take Doc more time to get rid of his properties the way he was doing it, but it was safer. There was nothing to do but wait. And he was good at that.

* * * * *

Two men with black wool ski caps pulled over their heads silently climbed down the ladder to the fire escape. Frankie's apartment was on the sixth floor, so they didn't have far to climb. Tommy removed the suction cup from the shoulder bag he was carrying. He wet the rim with spit and stuck it to the window, then cut a circle in the glass and gently popped it out. He handed it to his brother, then reached in, unlatched the catch and eased the window open. He switched on his flashlight and climbed into the apartment through the window with his brother behind him. Tommy walked into the hall and noticed that the bedroom door was slightly ajar. "Tommy, I hope she's naked so it'll be easy to get some pussy," Lester whispered.

"Shut up, stupid," Tommy whispered back as he opened the door. The blankets were rumpled up on the bed. Lester rushed over and threw himself on top of the mattress and wrestled the blankets off. The bed was empty.

Tommy rolled his eyes at his brother. "Check the bathroom, idiot," he whispered

Lester walked into the hallway and checked the bathroom

and the spare room, but both were empty.

"Where the hell is she?" Tommy demanded.

"How should I know? Maybe she went to a party or a bar. Who knows?" Lester stood with his hands on his hips, and looked around the apartment.

"We're here now, so we might as well wait until she gets back. You take the first watch. Wake me in two hours," Tommy ordered.

"Why is it that you're first all the time? Who made you the boss?" Lester complained.

"Who's the oldest?"

"You are, Tommy, but..."

His brother interrupted him. "But nothing. Who got better grades in school? I did, so that makes me the smartest. Now do what I told you."

"Okay, okay, you probably cheated anyway," Lester mumbled.

"Look, you can get mad if you want to, but we haven't done so badly with me doing the thinking. We're doing this job, and if we do this right, it could mean that we can move up to the serious money. If we screw up, you can go back to pushing a broom."

"I know, Tommy, but sometimes I'd like to be the boss.

* * * * *

Tommy woke with a start as daylight crept in through the rip in the window shade. He got out of bed and pulled up the shade, letting the morning light spread across the room. It was eight-fifteen by his watch.

"Les!" he roared, feeling the anger begin to take hold of him. He tore open the bedroom door and ran into the small living room to find Lester asleep on the couch. He shook his brother violently. "Wake up, stupid! I can't trust you to do anything, can I?" he growled. Lester sat up and rubbed his eyes.

"What are you upset about?"

"You fell asleep, you damned fool. You were supposed to wake me up!"

Lester stood. He was a few inches taller than his older brother.

"You were sleeping so soundly it would have been a shame to wake you. Try to be a nice guy and this is what I get," Lester mumbled.

"Suppose she came in while we were sleeping, then what?" Tommy said red-faced.

"Well she didn't come home last night. Probably shacked up somewhere. Check the door safety locks."

Tommy checked the door and saw that Lester was right. "See what I told you, she never came home," Les said confidently.

"Les, that's not the point. The point is that she could have come home and found us sleeping. Do you understand what I'm saying?"

"You're right for the first time."

"That was not very professional of you. You're going to have to get your act together from now on."

"I will. I promise. What do we do now?" Les sat back down on the sofa and rested his chin in his hands, looking to Tommy more like a 12-year-old boy waiting for his school lesson than a hired kidnapper.

Tommy thought for a minute. "We'll use her phone to call Mr. Epstein and let him know how we made out. Then we wait. She has to be home some time."

Four hours hour passed and there was still no sign of Frankie. Lester went into the kitchen and pulled the refrigerator door open. Except for a leftover TV dinner and two bottles of beer, the refrigerator was empty. "What's in there? I'm starving," Tommy said.

"Nothing but two bottles of beer," Lenny said, handing Tommy one of the bottles. Their wait was in vain --- by six o'clock it was obvious Frankie was not coming home. Tommy called Mr. Epstein to let him know what had happened. They would stay until evening, and if she didn't show up, they would check the store where she worked with her mother.

Lester hung up. "We can watch the house from the car. At least we can get something to eat."

"What if someone sees us on the fire escape?" Tommy asked his brother.

"Well, then we'll just go out the front door. For now, I just want to call my girlfriend."

"I said no more calls, let's go," Tommy ordered.

"I said I'm going to call Cheryl before we go," Lester insisted.

Tommy grabbed the phone from his brother and ripped the wire out of the wall. "I said no more calls," he repeated, and threw the phone on the bed.

* * * * *

Tommy sat in the car watching the building while Lester went to a deli to get a couple of sandwiches and beer. It was midnight, and Frankie still had not returned. "I don't think she's coming back here anymore," Tommy said, checking his watch. "We'll check the store in the morning, but if you ask me, she split for good."

Lester took the last swig of beer and yawned.

* * * * *

It was almost nine o' clock the next morning when Tommy and Lester reached the store. "How are we going to handle this? Should I knock the old lady around?" Lester asked eagerly

"No violence, you understand! You let me handle this. All you have to do is go along with what I say. And don't screw up," Tommy warned. Both men entered the shop and found Sophie alone. Laurie would not be there for another hour.

"Excuse me, ma'am," Tommy said, "but I'm looking for Frankie."

"I thought I knew all of Frankie's friends," Sophie said, smiling kindly at the two men.

"Well, we're from out of town. Frankie said that if we were ever up this way we should look her up."

"Oh," Sophie said. "Well, you're too late. She left three days ago. She said that this town was getting too dull for her and she just left. You know Frankie; she was always the restless type." Sophie looked at the two men curiously. "Where did you say you met Frankie?"

Tommy hesitated. "Uh, Brooklyn, we met her in Brooklyn. When will she be coming back?"

"Who knows?" Sophie said, raising her hands up to the ceiling. The men excused themselves and left. Sophie looked up at the ceiling after they left, speaking to the empty room. "Dear God, it finally rubbed off on me. Only three weeks with my daughter and already she has taught me to lie. But, God, I do not believe they were Fran's friends. I think maybe they were up to no good. So you can forgive me this one time. Thank you God."

* * * * *

Tommy and Les spent half the day watching the store, but

in the long run they came to the same conclusion as before ---
that Frankie had left New York for parts unknown. Tommy
called Mr. Epstein to tell him what had happened and to get
some guidance. He told him they could stay and ask around
some more, but that it would be a waste of time and money.
Doc was reluctant, but he agreed with Tommy. Doc himself
would never really be happy until he knew Frankie was dead.
Maybe he was really lucky. Maybe she was gone forever.

PART TWO

CHAPTER EIGHT

THE PROPOSITION

Frankie and Ricardo had just finished a late breakfast. All through the meal, it seemed to Frankie that Ricardo had something to say, but he seemed reluctant to speak. Frankie brushed the hair back from his face with one hand and looked into his eyes. "Ricardo, you seem to be very pre-occupied. Is there something you want to say? Out with it," Frankie said sweetly.

"Yes, there is something I want to say, but I feel foolish."

"Just say it Ricardo."

"Did you really mean what you said last night?"

"What did I say last night?" she asked playfully.

"Frankie, you are making fun of me. You said you would marry me."

Frankie's emotions were mixed. That's why she needed to talk to Midge. "I'm sorry, Ricardo. I was just teasing you. Yes, I said I would, and I meant it."

"Frankie, I meant what I said about my proposition."

"All I want out of you is your love and respect. The rest is unimportant. Because without these things I will have nothing," Frankie said sincerely. She got up and walked around the table and sat on Ricardo's lap. She kissed him gently. "If I ever catch you cheating on me, you're a dead man," Frankie said with a playful smile. "Can you handle that part of the bargain?"

Ricardo put his arm on her waist and loosened the ties of her robe. "Mi querida, you are not wearing any clothes under your robe. The servants will see you like that," he said blushing.

"You know, for a man in your business, someone people fear, *mi querido*, you're a pussycat," Frankie said, and nibbled on his earlobe.

"I must admit I am, as they say, putty in your hands. But I must insist that you be more conservative."

Frankie tightened the belt of her robe and walked back to her seat. She did not know what was wrong with her. She had never acted like this before.

Ricardo looked at Frankie's face and saw the tears welling up in her eyes. "I have hurt your feelings," he said sadly. Frankie fled to the house, the tears streaming down her cheeks.

* * * * *

Frankie lay on the bed wiping her tears with the collar of her robe. *What's wrong with me? Why am I acting like a fool? I wish Midge were here.* All Frankie knew was that she hurt inside. She was not aware of the time she had lain on the bed, but she was awakened by a commotion in the corridor and a pounding on her door. She sat up as the door opened and Midge came in. "Midge!" Frankie cried out and jumped off the bed to hug her dearest friend. "Oh, Midge! I'm so happy you're here. I don't know what to do."

Midge stepped back and looked her friend over. "If that son of a bitch hurt you, I'll cut his nuts off," she said, slashing through the air with an imaginary knife.

"No, it's not that. I think there is something wrong with me."

They both walked out onto the porch, Midge's arm around Frankie's waist, and sat down. "Okay, honey. Start from the beginning. Spill."

Frankie told Midge about Ricardo's proposition and about

her actions after everything was over. She tried to explain to Midge how crazy she felt inside and how she hated Ricardo, but loved him at the same time.

Midge listened silently and handed Frankie her handkerchief. "So, that's it," Midge said. "Well, my dear friend. The tightness in your chest and the confusion you feel, I never thought I would see the day."

"See what day?" Frankie asked angrily.

"Temper, temper," Midge said smugly. "You're in love, and you're trying to fight it. That's all it is." Midge grabbed Frankie's hands. "Good catch."

"But I don't really know him that long." Frankie sounded confused.

"Look, that's the way it happens. If you'd gotten laid more often, you would understand the process better."

Frankie smiled. "I'm in love. I'm in love. I'm in love," she repeated. "That's it. There's nothing wrong with me."

"I'm afraid so," Midge said in her mother hen voice. "Now take a shower and you'll feel better. I'll wait down stairs for you."

* * * * *

Ricardo stood as Midge walked out onto the patio. "Is she all right, Señorita?" he asked uncertainly. "I am worried about her."

"She'll be fine," Midge said and took a seat.

"Her behavior worried me. One second we were talking, then she started to cry," Ricardo threw his hands up in exasperation.

"Well, not to worry. Old Midge fixed the problem," she said, smoothing a white linen napkin over her lap. "The kid is in love, and didn't know it. And you, my friend, as long as you never break her heart, you will have a long and happy life."

"Do me a favor ---stop calling me Señorita. Just plain Midge will do. You got anything to drink around here?"

"I am sorry, Señorita. I mean Midge. Maria," Ricardo called out. Maria quickly came out to the patio. "Yes, Señor?"

"Bring the Señorita Midge something to drink," he ordered.

"Two bottles of beer, Maria, and thank you," Midge said, and watched the maid disappear back into the house. She turned to Ricardo. "You may know a lot about Frankie in your files. But you don't know Frankie as a person. Frankie has not had very much experience with men, and what little she has had is not worth talking about. But who's perfect? Certainly not you and definitely not me. But she has never been in love. Yeah, she's streetwise. But she is not love-wise. You were married once. You should understand all this."

"That may be part of the problem, Midge," he said. "My marriage was pre-arranged. Love didn't enter into it of my free will. We were two people who just got used to each other. Do not misunderstand me. I grew to love my wife, as I am sure she did me, but Frankie is the only woman I have been with or have ever desired to be with since my wife died. She brings out the passion in me. I do love her." Ricardo looked ready to blush.

"Ricardo, just give her time. She has never had to deal with love. I am sure it will all work out."

"Thank you, Midge. Now I know why Francine thinks so highly of you. And I am happy that you are her friend."

"Did she tell you to call her Francine?"

"Yes. She said that if we were going to be married, that is what I should call her."

"It must be love. Wonders never cease," Midge said with surprise. Maria returned with a two beers and a glass on a tray and set them down before Midge, who gave the maid a thank you smile.

"There is one thing I should tell you. Frankie loves you and she is a one-man woman," Midge said, pouring the brew into her glass. "And I honestly think you will never have any regrets about marrying her. She may drive you crazy, but she will love you with all her heart. But, if you ever two-time her, she is quite capable of cutting your heart out. And you will also have to deal with me, because I'll be helping her!" Midge said, raising her glass to Ricardo.

"I do not have to say this. But I will tell you that I would never hurt Francine for any reason at all. I fell in love with her the first time I saw her."

"What about the trouble we have with Doc?"

"This is something I want to speak with her about."

"Speak with me about what?" Frankie called out as she stepped onto the patio. Ricardo started to stand. Frankie rested her hands on his shoulders and sat on his lap.

Ricardo put his arms around Frankie's waist and looked into her eyes. "*Mi Querida,* I am sorry about what happened before. I did not mean to upset you."

Frankie kissed him twice, forgetting Midge was there.

Midge interrupted. "You guys want me to leave?"

Frankie laughed. "No, silly."

She kissed Ricardo once more, and sat in the chair next to Midge. Ricardo looked at Frankie with her dark hair pinned up in a bun, and loved the way she smiled when she was amused about something. The red outfit she wore complemented her tan. Midge had made Ricardo realize that he knew nothing about women and even less about love. He only knew that this woman, who went to great lengths to let him know that she was no lady, was all that she said she was not. She had his heart. And that would last forever. He considered Midge to be a diamond in the rough.

"Ricardo, if we're boring you I'm sorry," Frankie said.

"No, *mi querida,* I was just thinking that I am very happy that you are feeling better."

"What is it you wanted to talk about?"

"It can wait till tomorrow, but tonight, in honor of our guest, I think we should go out for dinner."

Midge protested. "Ricardo, I didn't bring any clothes, except what I am wearing. When I was told that Frankie needed me, I just came as fast as I so didn't pack a thing."

"Well, in that case ladies, we will close the restaurant down to the public and have our dinner. And tomorrow Antonio will take you both shopping."

"Miguel, attend to this. Tell them dinner at eight," Ricardo ordered.

Midge grabbed Frankie's hand. "Baby, if you don't marry this guy I will."

"Over my dead body you will." Frankie joked, but she was dead serious.

* * * * *

Frankie lay next to Ricardo, listening to his quiet breathing. *Midge was right --- the tightness in my chest is gone.* She shook her lover awake.

"*Mi querida,* what is wrong?" he said turning to her.

"Nothing," she said, kissing him. She just wanted to feel safe in his arms.

* * * * *

Since Frankie had arrived, his early breakfasts had turned into late breakfasts. "Antonio," he called out after swallowing a bite of toast.

"Yes, Señor Montoya. "

"Sit down. I wish to talk with you."

In all the years he had worked for Ricardo Montoya, only once did he remember his boss asking him to sit with him. Antonio was worried. "Have I done something to offend you, Señor?"

Ricardo smiled. "No Antonio. On the contrary, I have a job of great importance for you. But first I must ask you a question. I trust you with my life, so you must be honest with me. Even if you think I will be angry with your answer."

"I swear on my life to tell you the truth. "

"Antonio. Do you like Señorita Francine? Do you think that because of my age marrying her would be wrong?"

Antonio sighed in relief. "Yes, I think the Señorita would be very good for you. She has already taken you out of your shell, and yes, I do like her."

"That is good to hear, because I am putting the life of the woman I love in your hands. You will keep her out of harm's way. You will be her constant companion. All this I entrust to you. You have been loyal to me. Now you must take care of her. Will you do this for me?" Ricardo could see Antonio's chest swell with pride.

"Señor Montoya, I am honored that you pick me for this position. I will guard the Señorita with my life. She will never be out of my sight. May I ask who you will select for my position?" Antonio asked.

"Do you have anyone in mind, Antonio?"

"Yes, Señor, I do."

"Would that be your brother, Eduardo?"

"Yes it would be, Señor."

"Then it is done. He will take your place."

"I will miss working with Miguel," Antonio said sadly.

Ricardo laughed. "Miguel will continue to work with you. I

have the feeling that it will take the two of you to look after Francine."

* * * * *

Breakfast was over, and the three of them sat sipping coffee. "Now, *mi querida*, I have something of great importance to speak with you about," Ricardo said sternly to Frankie.

"Guess it's time for me to take a swim," Midge said as she started to stand.

"No," Ricardo said. "I would like you to stay."

"This must be a winner." Frankie teased.

"Because we will be married in a few weeks, I must ask you to give up looking for Doc."

Frankie started to say something, but Ricardo stopped her. "Please, Francine, let me finish. I will find him and he will be punished. If you wish to be there when I find him, you may, but it is much too dangerous for you to pursue this matter any more." Ricardo braced himself for an argument.

"If you honor your promise to me about quitting this business, then I will do as you ask, that is, as long as it is not an order," Frankie came back.

"The transition will take at least six months. I have made you a promise, and I will do this for you."

Ricardo was at a loss for words. For once, Frankie had not been stubborn or argued with him. Somehow, he knew she was not being truthful.

"There is one more thing. Antonio and Miguel will be your constant companions. They will take you anywhere you want to go. If there is anything you want Antonio will see to your needs."

"I don't need a bodyguard. I can take care of myself,"

Frankie protested.

"I am quite sure you are capable of taking care of yourself. Nevertheless, we will let Antonio take that burden from you. There will be no more discussion about this matter."

Realizing this was an argument she could not win, Frankie gave in. "I would like to go back to New York to see if my mother and sister will come to the wedding."

"When would you like to leave, Frankie?" Ricardo asked.

"Would tomorrow be all right? I will only be away for a few days," Frankie answered. "Midge has to go back to Miami anyway."

"That is not a problem. Antonio will drive you home."

"Ricardo, does he have to come with us?" Frankie said.

"Frankie, you promised there would be no arguing about this."

"But, Ricardo, please," Frankie whined.

"No, and that is final."

"Oh, all right. Midge and I are going down by the lake for some girl talk. We'll see you later."

When the ladies left the table, Ricardo called for Antonio. "I have reason to believe that Frankie may try to slip away from you. Keep an eye on both of them when you get to New York."

"What makes you think so, Señor Montoya?"

"Simple, Antonio. She gave in too easily."

* * * * *

"What's up with you? Has getting laid every night dulled your senses?" Midge gave Frankie a light punch in the arm as they walked.

"If he thinks he has me tamed and that I no longer have any fight left in me because I'm in love, Ricardo will not suspect that I am going to try anything," Frankie bragged.

"What about Antonio? He'll be hard to shake."

"I need some time to figure out how to get rid of Antonio."

"Speaking of Antonio, he's some hunk of a man," Midge said with a wink. "I wouldn't mind putting my shoes under *his* bed. Meow!"

"I was wondering when you would get around to him."

"I'm in no hurry."

"Down girl, down," Frankie said, laughing.

"You know, Frankie, this time I agree with Ricardo. Let *them* find Doc and take care of business. You got a good thing going. Why mess it up?"

"No, I can't. If anybody finds that bastard, it's going to be me."

"You should really listen to Ricardo and give this up," Midge pressured.

"Does that mean you're not going to help me?" Frankie stopped and looked closely at her friend.

"Hell, yes, I'm going to help you. Karen will be home in three weeks. They're giving her a break before her final operation to keep her from getting depressed. We can do the old airport switch like we planned for Doc," Midge grinned.

"You're a genius, dear girl." Frankie said.

"I know, I know!"

* * * * *

The trip to New York was uneventful. They went straight to Frankie's apartment, and Antonio led the way up the stairs. On the top of the stairs, Antonio put his hand out for the women to stop. The door was wide open. Antonio pulled out his Beretta and put his fingers to his lips, telling them to keep quiet. Then he waved Miguel into the apartment. The two men checked every room, but all was quiet. In few minutes, Antonio came back out into the hallway. "Whoever they are, they have gone. The apartment is empty," Antonio said with relief.

Frankie noticed the two empty beer bottles and picked one up. "They drank my beer," she said with disgust.

Midge went into the bedroom. "The phone wire was ripped out of the wall. Looks to me like someone spent the night here."

"Antonio, could you please check the roof?" Frankie asked. She pointed to the window. "I think they came in through there." Antonio crawled through the open window onto the fire escape leading to the roof, while Miguel stayed with the women.

"Midge," Frankie said, "do you still have that cop friend?"

"Yes, I do. Why?"

"I don't think this was a robbery. I think someone waited here for me to come home. And I think they used the phone." She heard Antonio climbing onto the fire escape. "Ask him to get a list of numbers called from here this week," she said, as Antonio came back through the window. "Except for the piece of glass cut from the window, there's no clue to who the thieves are."

"Well, it doesn't matter in any event. There wasn't much to steal anyway. Let's go," Frankie said nonchalantly. Antonio's orders were to report all incidents, no matter how unimportant they seemed. Ricardo Montoya knew his future wife better than she thought he did. He expected her to try to elude Antonio, and he was pretty sure she would succeed.

* * * * *

Frankie walked into the store, followed by Midge and Antonio, while Miguel stayed in the limo. Laurie was taking inventory. "Hello, Laurie. Where's Momma?" Frankie asked cheerfully.

"You finally decided to return," Laurie snipped. She eyed Antonio and Midge as Frankie walked past her into the back room.

"Momma," Frankie said happily and hugged her mother. "Momma, I know I've been gone longer then I said I would be, but please don't be mad at me. Anyway, when I tell you my secret you're going to be so happy you won't have any time to be mad."

"So, what is this big secret of yours?" Sophie was suspicious.

"Momma, I am going to get married in two weeks and I want you to come to my wedding."

"And who is this mystery man that has swept you off your feet?" Sophie sounded doubtful.

"Have you ever heard of Ricardo Montoya?"

"Frankie, he is one of the richest men in the world. Is this one of your stories?"

"No, Momma, it's true. I even have a bodyguard. Come, I'll show you." Frankie took her mother by the hand. "Come with me." She dragged her mother out of the store and pointed to Antonio. "Here he is. This is Antonio."

Antonio bowed. "It is an honor to meet you, Señora." Antonio gently grabbed Sophie's hand and kissed it. The older woman smiled and blushed.

Laurie stepped forward. "I'm Frankie's sister, Laura," she said, waiting for her hand to be kissed. Antonio only bowed. "It is a pleasure to meet you also," he said politely. Laura looked crushed.

Sophie looked up at Antonio. "Is all this true, young man? Is she really getting married?"

Antonio cleared his throat nervously. "Yes, it is true, and I have been ordered by Señor Montoya to see to it that Señorita Frankie is always safe."

Frankie put an arm around Midge's shoulders. "Of course, Momma you already know Midge."

Midge smiled and nodded her head.

Sophie walked over to Midge. "I have never liked you, but then I never really took the time to know you. So I now thank you for taking care of my daughter." Midge was at a loss for words, never expecting such kind words from a woman who disliked her so much.

"I wonder if you would let me use your phone," was all Midge could think to say.

"Yes it's inside," Sophie replied.

Midge went to the back room, picked up the phone and dialed Detective Jerry Delaine's number. When he got on the line, she didn't hesitate. Would he do her a favor, for old times sake, she asked, promising to take care of him, as she had some free time. "I'll call you back in an hour," she said and hung up. She walked back through the curtains to the front of the store in time to hear Frankie say, "Momma will you come to the wedding?"

"I will speak to your father and see what he says."

"Why ask him, Momma? You know what he's going to say."

"I am sorry Fran, but I can't change him overnight," her mother replied curtly.

"So that means you're not coming. I thought it was too good to be true," Frankie said tearfully.

"Please, I do not wish to talk about this any more today," her mother said.

"No matter what you decide to do, Momma, I'll still love you," Frankie said and walked out of the store.

* * * * *

They stopped at a local diner and, after ordering grilled cheese sandwiches and a chocolate shake each, Midge excused herself to make a call.

"Hi, sweet thing, you got anything for me? No Jerry, I don't want to tell you anything about it. I'm doing a friend a favor, okay? Hold on a second," Midge said into the phone while she rummaged around in her bag for a pen and something to write on. "Let me write that down." She took down the information on the back of an old business card.

"Thanks, sweet thing," she laughed playfully. "Yeah, you know how that turns me on. I can't wait to see you later."

Midge hung up and returned to the table, giving Frankie the thumbs up sign. Frankie grinned from ear to ear.

"Señorita, is there anything else you would like to do or see before we go back home?" Antonio queried.

"Midge, how about you, you got anything to do?"

"No, not if you don't."

"No, Antonio. Let's go home."

* * * * *

Sophie went to the back room to straighten out the stock for the day. She expected Frankie to tell her what a hard woman she was, but what did kids know about tradition? They had everything they wanted. They had choices she never had. How much did they know or care about her life? She was a simple farm girl, one of four sisters who worked on their father's dairy farm. She did not choose Aaron and he did not choose her. Their marriage was made before they were born. She would admit if she could, that love was never a factor in these matches. Through the years, she had learned to like then respect her husband. She was brought up believing that the husband's word was law. What did her children know about being persecuted first by the Communists? Maybe it was good that they did not know of these things, maybe it was not. Sophie was not sure. Frankie had told her it was time to move into the twentieth century.

Sophie turned as Laura entered the room. "Before you say anything, Laurie, I have decided to go to Frankie's wedding. And I have also decided that your father will go whether he wants to or not and, you my dear daughter, and so will you and your husband." Sophie was not about to back down.

Laura hugged her mother. "Yes, Momma, if you say so. I love you, but I think you have lost your mind to actually defy Poppa."

* * * * *

Ricardo was in his study when Frankie returned. Excited to be back on the compound, she rushed past Eduardo and opened the study door. "Ricardo, I'm back! Ricardo? Oh, I'm sorry. I didn't know you were busy." She suddenly noticed the two men sitting on the opposite side of the room on the leather sofa.

Ricardo stood up. "It's all right. We were just finishing up, *mi querida*. Gentlemen, this lovely flower is my future wife, Francine," he said, circling an arm around Frankie's waist.

Both men, dressed in sharp navy blue suits, stood to greet her. "Francine, this is Louis Vargas and Jesus Arroyo, business acquaintances of mine."

Both men bowed in Frankie's direction as they left the room.

Frankie put her arms around Ricardo and kissed him passionately. "I never thought I would say this, but I missed you and I missed being here." They walked out to the patio, and Frankie felt like a teenager on her first date.

* * * * *

After an early supper, Ricardo announced that he had some other visitors coming and that he would be busy for an hour or so. Later, when the same two men returned with them, they resumed their meeting.

As I told you gentleman earlier," Ricardo said, "I have decided to retire. I have already picked my successor and he has been approved by the board. Between now and the time I get married, the transition will be completed. But I will be available for any counseling that may arise."

But Ricardo, are you sure this is what you want?" Jesus asked.

"Yes. I have been in the organization more than half of my life, and now it's time for me to take life easy and enjoy my wife and future children," Ricardo announced.

* * * * *

Frankie and Midge took their usual walk down to the lake, with Antonio not far behind them. "Well, what did you find out? I've been dying to ask you all day," Frankie pressed.

"You don't know what I had to promise this guy for this information," Midge cracked.

"I don't think I want to know, so don't tell me."

"There were a lot of local calls, but there was one long distance call to a Mr. Aaron Epstein in Vermont. I have the address," Midge said, handing the business card to Frankie.

"This has to be him. I can feel it. I knew he would slip up. I got him now," Frankie said, crumpling the card in her clenched fist.

"Why don't you just give the card to Ricardo and let him take care of it?" Midge pleaded.

"No, this bastard is mine, all mine."

"I thought you would say that. It would be too easy to let Ricardo handle things, and you don't do things the easy way," Midge said angrily.

"You don't have to help me anymore. I'll understand. You've done more than I expected you to do."

"No, I said I would help you and I will. But, I want to be there with you when you nail him."

"No. You've been a good friend. And, besides, you have your part to do. That's going to be hard enough. If anything happens to me, give the card to Ricardo and tell him I love him."

"Why do you have to be so damned stubborn all the time?" Midge huffed.

Frankie smiled at Midge. "That's what makes me so loveable."

"I could say if I don't come with you, I'll tell Ricardo."

"You wouldn't do that, would you?"

"No, damn it. You know I wouldn't."

* * * * *

Antonio stood in front of Ricardo's desk. "You wish to see me, Señor."

"Yes, Antonio. Did all go well on this trip? Were there any signs of a conspiracy?"

"No, Señor. All went well." Antonio said hesitantly.

"I sense that there is something you are not telling me."

"I do not know if it is my place to make this comment on your future wife's family, or maybe I do not understand the way *gringos* think," Antonio said.

Ricardo looked at him and nodded his head. "Sit, Antonio, and tell me what is bothering you about Francine's family."

Antonio cleared his throat. "Things were going well until she met with her mother and the Señorita asked her to come to her wedding. Her mother refused to come," Antonio added nervously.

"And is this because of me?" Ricardo was curious.

"No, Señor. She was delighted that it was you. It seemed that the father has decided never to speak to his daughter again, but I do not know why. It did make the Señorita cry; that is all I know."

Ricardo seemed to be in thought when Antonio spoke. "Señor, I do not wish to anger you. But you have put the protection of Señorita Frankie in my hands and, well..." Antonio cleared his throat again.

"Out with it." Ricardo demanded.

"I feel like a school boy bringing home tales to my mother."

Ricardo laughed. "I understand, but this is part of your job Antonio, it is important that I know everything for now. I am still afraid that the Señorita may do something rash about finding Doc, and I want to be ready. I would not ask this of you if it were not important."

"Thank you for your understanding, Señor. "

* * * * *

That night, Frankie lay in Ricardo's arms. "*Mi querida, Frankie,* what is wrong? You seem to be a million miles from here. Do I bore you already?"

"No, it's not you, it's me. I will never bored of you. I was just thinking. Forget about it."

"You will have to tell me, or I will put you over my knee

and spank you."

Frankie playfully bit his ear and said in her sexiest voice "You promise, baby?"

"Frankie, you are incorrigible." They both laughed and then lay in silence for a few minutes. *"Mi querida,* please tell me what is wrong," Ricardo said at last.

"My mother will not come to the wedding because my father hates me." Tearfully, Frankie told Ricardo the whole story, including what he already knew. Ricardo was more comfortable now that he knew the whole story. He cradled her in his arms as she cried herself to sleep. "Who knows, my darling? These things have a way of working themselves out. If not, I may be able to fix this matter." Ricardo kissed her cheek as she slept.

* * * * *

"You know, Momma, in the past I really treated Fran like dirt, but you are telling me the truth about Fran. I have to admire her now," Laura admitted, as she dusted the store's shelves. "She ruined her life so that her father would not disown his son. You really hurt her by not telling him. Isn't it time he knew the truth?"

"He knows the truth already, but he will not believe it's true, because he doesn't want to." Sophie said sadly. "I was brought up believing that the man was the boss. There was no free choice in my marriage. Our parents made the match for us. We had no free will in these matters. So, at my age, change comes slow. But it does come."

"I know, Momma, and I know you will do what is right. If you need me by your side, I will be there for you," Laura said.

Sophie smiled at her eldest daughter.

"Momma, what did the Doctor say about Poppa's health?"

Laura asked.

"The doctor said he could come back to work in six months if he continues to take it easy now."

"Don't forget to tell Poppa that Fran has been here helping you out, but you don't have to mention that she took off for three weeks," Laura said.

Sophie looked at Laura quizzically. "Since when did I become the pupil and you the teacher?"

* * * * *

Theo had never met Karen, so he felt a bit silly waiting for her flight to empty out through the exit door, and standing there with a sign in his hand saying Midge's party was waiting for her. Karen spotted Theo, who towered over everyone, right away as she came through the gate. She introduced herself and asked Theo why Midge had not shown up herself.

Still feeling awkward, Theo explained why Midge could not be there and that there was a letter waiting for her at the villa that would explain everything. He had promised Midge to stick around long enough to meet Karen and get her settled. It amazed him how much she looked like Frankie.

Theo explained to Karen that he was flying home to Jamaica next week, and told her that there would be a servant around to take care of her until Midge returned.

Karen thanked Theo, and asked if he wanted her to drive him to the airport. "If I can get you there I can always find my way back."

* * * * *

Karen sat in the lounge chair sipping her seven and seven while she read Midge's letter. Everything was still on. Midge instructed Karen to sit tight and to stay out of the hot Florida sun as much as possible --- or wear plenty of sunscreen.

Three days passed when Midge finally called and elaborated on the plan. There was a suitcase in the hall closet, with everything Karen needed, and other instructions.

* * * * *

Karen looked at her naked body in the bathroom's full-length mirror, and admired the work the surgeons had done on her. She was not being vain. It was the first time in years that she could look at herself nude and not cry. She had retreated into her own little world, knowing how hideous they had made her look, and trying to forget the horror in Eric's eyes when he looked at her naked body. That look had haunted her. If the man who said he loved her looked at her that way, how would someone who didn't know or love her react? It was true that he had said he was sorry, but it was the look on his face that lingered in her mind. She pushed her hair to the side and looked at her scarred face. After all these years, the scars would be gone. She would no longer have to be ashamed of the way she looked.

There wasn't much else to do but wait. She wondered what life would be like, now that she could live normally. She had Ricardo Montoya to thank for all this. She wanted to thank him personally, if she ever got the chance to.

* * * * *

Midge announced that she would have to leave in a few days, but that she would be back in time for the wedding. Frankie wanted to have a small affair --- just family and some close friends --- but there seemed to be a disagreement on that, and where she and Ricardo should get married. Ricardo wanted to be married in Spain at the chapel where he was baptized. Frankie didn't want to argue about this, because she had never been very religious anyway. But she still wanted to try to please her parents and marry in the synagogue, even though they would not attend the wedding.

"Listen, no more arguments." Midge said, taking a deep breath. "I have everything figured out for the both of you. "First you get married at the synagogue, then, after the reception, both of you go to Spain and get married in the church, and everyone is happy."

"But I am not of the Jewish faith!" Ricardo said frustrated.

"The Rabbi is a good friend of mine, so don't worry about the trivial matters." Midge said sounding sheepish.

"You really get around, don't you?" Frankie said. Midge started to say something. Frankie stopped her saying, "No, please I don't want to know why he owes you a favor."

Ricardo looked at her in amazement, saying, "Can we do anything to keep you here until the wedding?" Ricardo asked.

"No. I'm sorry, but I really have to go. I have some business in Miami that I can't put off, but I'll be back in plenty of time. I wouldn't miss this wedding for the world!"

CHAPTER NINE

THE SWITCH

Frankie spent the morning with Midge helping her pack her suitcases. Ricardo was in the city on business, so they had plenty of time to talk. "Where is Antonio now?" Midge asked.

"He's usually in the kitchen with Maria when he doesn't have to watch me."

"Too bad for her. Frankie, I decided something. I'm going to marry that guy when this is over," Midge said positively.

"What guy are you talking about?" Frankie was confused.

"Antonio, silly."

"Midge, you're crazy, but all I can say is poor Antonio." They both laughed.

"You know what to do now?" Midge asked, changing the subject.

"I can do this in my dreams."

"I hate to sound like a bitch, but we are only going to get one chance at this. If we screw up, Karen and I wind up going to Miami again and you wind up behind the eight ball, and we will never get another chance, Ricardo will see to that," Midge warned.

"The one good thing that comes out of this, no matter what happens, is I came with the clothes on my back and thanks to Ricardo, I go back with three bags of clothes," Midge bragged.

"You know, after this is over, I'm going to give this Maria a run for her money," Midge said playfully.

"I feel sorry for the poor guy after you finish with him," Frankie joked. "By the way, where is Karen now?"

"She should have landed at JFK about an hour ago. She's

staying at the Airport Hotel. She'll already be in the airport bathroom when we get there," Midge said.

"I'm going to have to ask Ricardo to come along with us, otherwise it won't look right. If he comes, no big deal. Nothing changes."

* * * * *

Karen arrived at JFK an hour later. She took a taxi to the hotel, showered and ordered a meal from room service. Midge said she would try to call her, but if for some reason she couldn't, the plan would remain the same. Karen was excited. The months of surgery and laying in bed was driving her crazy. The surgeons realized that if they didn't give her some time off before continuing with the operations, she would become depressed. This is what she needed --- some real excitement. When all the operations were finished, Midge said she was going to throw the biggest party anyone had ever seen.

* * * * *

Antonio loaded the bags early. Ricardo was sorry that he had business in the city and could not join them at the airport to see her off, but once again extended his offer for Midge to stay until the wedding. Ricardo gulped down a cup of coffee and kissed Frankie goodbye. "I did not realize I was running late. *Mi querida*, do you see what you have done to me? I am always late for appointments." He kissed Frankie again.

"Eduardo, let us go," he ordered.

Frankie and Midge spent most of the morning relaxing, waiting for the time to pass. It was almost noon when Antonio came out to the patio and suggested an early lunch. Traffic can be unpredictable at times, he explained, and it would be a good idea if they left a little early. The women agreed.

"Would you care to join us for lunch, Antonio?" Frankie slyly asked.

"That is very kind, but it is not proper for me to do so. I must never do anything that puts the Señorita in danger. And sitting here with you, I am unable to do my job correctly."

"Let's see now," she said. "I can call you Antonio, but you can't call me Francine. You can take me shopping or to lunch, but you can't eat with me. This is really silly."

"I am sorry, but this is what is required of me by Señor Montoya. If I displease the Señorita, I will ask Señor Montoya to replace me with someone of your own choice. It was a great honor to be chosen as your bodyguard."

"No, Antonio," she said, taking his hands in hers. "I am pleased with Ricardo's choice. And I would not be happy if you quit. I trust you with my life, but this is all so new to me. I'll get used to it."

Antonio smiled. "I am sure you will get used to it."

Maria came onto the patio and asked Frankie and Midge what they would like for lunch.

"Do you have any more of that crab salad?" Midge asked.

"Yes, Señorita, we do," Maria replied.

"I'll have the same thing and a cup of tea, Marie," Frankie piped up.

"I think I will have something stronger. You sure you don't want anything stronger yourself?" Midge asked.

"No, my stomach feels queasy. I felt kind of nauseous this morning," Frankie complained. Living in these surroundings, she knew now how the other half lived. Time had gone by so fast she hardly realized that she had been here for almost three months. If she didn't feel better, she would go see a doctor.

"Too much late night skinny dipping with Rickie baby," Midge joked.

In spite of the tension, both women felt badly about lying to Ricardo, but they managed to hide it. The tea settled Frankie's stomach, and the morning was a pleasant one; Antonio had kept his distance, giving them as much privacy as they needed.

"You *are* coming to Spain with us for the wedding?" Frankie asked.

"There's no use in saying no, is there?"

"If you don't want to come, that's all right. I'll understand," Frankie said sadly.

"You have to be kidding. What would a wedding be if the maid of honor didn't show up?" Midge said laughing.

"That is, if there is going to be a wedding after he finds out what we've been planning."

"Don't worry; the man is hooked on you."

Antonio called out to them. "Señorita, it is time for us to leave."

"My, time goes by when you're having fun," Midge said.

Frankie's stomach was bothering her again. *Must be last minute jitters. God I hope Ricardo, forgives me.*

"Are you okay Frankie?" Midge asked, concerned. "You look a little green."

"I'm all right. I must have caught a cold."

"Antonio, please get her some ginger ale."

Frankie drank the ginger ale and it seemed to settle her stomach somewhat. *Must be the jitters,* she thought again.

The limo met them as they walked down the wide steps, and Frankie glanced at the front of the house with its marble columns.

"Antonio, I thought Ricardo took the limo this morning," Antonio smiled. "Señorita, there are four limos in the garage."

"Silly me," Frankie said embarrassed. "I have a lot to get used to."

The ride to the airport was a smooth and uneventful one. The limo eased to the curb and stopped. "Antonio, you and Miguel can go with the driver to park the limo after you unload the luggage," Frankie ordered.

"No, we cannot do that. The driver will know when to return for us."

"Well, I want you to go with him. I will not need you until it's time to go," she said as authoritatively as she could.

"I am sorry. My orders are not to leave you and not to let you out of my sight."

Frankie pouted. "Do I have to order you to do what I want?"

"Señor Montoya gave me strict orders to stay by your side at all times. He told me he had an idea that something may go wrong today. And no matter what you say, I was not to leave you."

Both women walked through the double doors, out of earshot from Antonio.

"Midge, do you think he's onto us?"

"I think your Ricardo is one hell of a slick guy."

"What do we do now?" Frankie asked.

"We go ahead with our plan. He knows you're going to run, but not when."

"I love the challenge. I can feel my adrenaline flowing."

Frankie turned to Antonio and tried to gain his confidence. "I am sorry. I didn't know about your orders."

An announcement stated that United Flight 764 was leaving for Miami in fifteen minutes.

"Damn it," Midge said aloud.

"What's wrong?" Frankie asked.

"I have to go to the bathroom."

"You scared me. Come on. I'll go with you. Antonio, after we come out of the bathroom, I want to walk Midge to the gate. Is it all right if you stay here as long as you can see me?" she asked. "Yes, Señorita. It will be all right."

Frankie and Midge hurried to the bathroom where Karen was waiting. The women laughed and hugged each other. They piled into the large handicap stall, where Frankie and Karen changed clothes and Frankie put on a blond wig. Karen handed Frankie a small suitcase and a shopping bag that held a very similar brown leather purse. From a distance, they looked alike. Frankie put her shoulder bag into the shopping bag and combed her hair down at the sides to look like Karen. "How do I look, girls?"

Midge checked her over once more. "You look fine. I'd better get going; I'll see you on the plane." The girls hugged each other one last time.

"Well, here I go." Frankie stopped and looked in the mirror for a second, and took a deep breath. Antonio saw a blond woman in blue jeans leave the washroom and head for the gate. She was handing her ticket to the attendant. He had seen her go in a few minutes before Frankie and Midge, but he thought that somehow she looked a little heavier. He dismissed the thought when Frankie and Midge came out of the bathroom. Midge waved as they both walked to the gate. The two women gave each other a last hug and Midge disappeared through the doorway. Frankie walked to the escalator without turning around.

Antonio realized that she was not coming back and panicked. "Señorita," he called out.

But Frankie paid no attention to him. He started after her, but she had already reached the ground level.

Antonio rushed down the escalator, pushing people aside. At the bottom, she disappeared. Antonio was in a state of panic, and pulled out his Beretta. He heard someone scream as he ran towards the baggage claims.

He yelled out to Frankie to stop and then he heard a voice: "Drop the gun, friend. You're under arrest." Antonio turned to see three policemen standing behind him, pointing their loaded guns at him.

"Put the gun down easy," one yelled.

Antonio lay the gun down and started to raise his hands over his head.

"Okay, put your hands behind your neck," the other officer ordered.

Antonio knew it was useless to resist. "Señor, I have diplomatic immunity," he called out.

"Likely story. Let's go, pal," one of the officers said as he started to cuff Antonio, who saw Frankie slip into the crowd.

"Stop her. She must not get away!" Antonio yelled.

"Let's go pal. Move it now!"

"Wait, please. Please check my top pocket."

The officer said. "No, you do it, but move very slow. If there's anything but a wallet in there..."

Antonio reached into his jacket pocket and pulled out a black identification folder showing he worked for the Spanish Embassy and had diplomatic immunity.

Antonio caught a glimpse of Frankie in the gathering crowd and pleaded with the officers. "Please, stop that woman."

"Okay, lady. Stop and come over here," the officer ordered.

Karen came obediently.

"What does she have to do with this?" the officer asked.

Antonio stopped talking. "They have switched women."

He grabbed Karen. "Where is she?" He yelled out.

"Hey, mister, let go. Officer, stop him. He's hurting me."

Antonio realized this woman was not Frankie, but she sure looked like her from a distance. "What did you do with her?" he demanded.

"Look, I don't know this lunatic. Can I go now?"

"Yeah, go ahead and get out of here."

Karen started to leave, then suddenly felt sorry for Antonio. "Hey you," she called out. Antonio turned to meet her gaze. She winked. "Don't worry... I am sure your friend is all right." She picked up her suitcase and disappeared into the crowd.

Antonio shook his head. The two women had conned him, and as if that wasn't enough, they had added insult to injury and rubbed his nose in it. The police asked him to explain what had happened for the report they would have to turn in.

Frankie and Midge toasted their success in their first class seats as the plane leveled off at ten thousand feet. The first stop would be Atlanta, where Midge would fly on to Miami, and Frankie would change flights and fly to Vermont. Their plane would reach Georgia at 2:10 p.m. Frankie's flight to Vermont would leave Atlanta at 2:41 p.m. and Midge's at 3:10 pm.

Karen took the next flight from JFK back to Miami. She'd have no problem, because no one was looking for her.

Both Frankie and Midge were sure that when the plane reached Miami someone would be there to greet her, so she had her story ready. They covered everything they could think of, even smuggling the gun past the security system. Knowing that her future husband always used his private jet to fly wherever they wanted to go, Frankie hoped she was right about Antonio's not knowing the airport security system. When Antonio got to the security system, Midge went through first then turned as Frankie entered. Just as the alarm went off, Frankie screamed and pretended to faint, falling forward. Antonio quickly stepped into the chamber to get her. In the confusion, Midge slipped the gun out of Frankie's shoulder bag. Antonio was stopped. Reaching into his jacket pocket to show his identification, Frankie pretended to be all right again. She held on to the booth and backed up, going through it again, and this time there was no alarm. She said she was all right and that it must have been the heat. Midge and an attendant helped Frankie to a seat.

* * * * *

They had never really been sure that their plan would work, so they were pleased with the way things had gone. They knew that Midge would be questioned when she reached Miami. Midge would tell them that Frankie got a line on Doc and he was somewhere in Washington, but that Frankie would not tell her where. That should keep them busy for a while. Once Frankie got to where she was gong, the rest would be easy. She would get her money and the diamonds, make the bastard suffer for what he did, then just kill him, go home and get married. She thought about Ricardo, and for a second thought about calling him when she reached her destination to let him know she was all right. She knew that as long as she didn't talk too long, he couldn't trace the call. *Well, Ricardo,* she though, *I told you life with me would be interesting. Now you know I wasn't telling you a lie.*

* * * * *

Her plane landed at the small airport on time. She had no luggage to claim, so she was out of the airport and in her rental car in record time. She drove until she found a suitable hotel, and explained to the clerk that she had no credit card. Frankie paid in advance for two weeks' rental in cash. At a local Wal-Mart, she bought some clothes and a carry-on suitcase, and headed back to her motel for a shower and bite to eat. She had his name and address. All she needed were directions. Frankie was confident that she would conclude her business and be on her way home in a matter of a few days.

* * * * *

Frankie was up early the next morning. She sat on the edge of the bed, yawned and stretched. She felt good --- the first morning in more than a week that the queasiness was replaced by hunger.

After a shower Frankie changed into a pair of jeans and a halter-top, and stopped at the chamber of commerce to get some maps of the area. She was unable to get a street map and the ones she *did* get were mostly for tourist information. She stopped at a sporting goods store and bought a pair of binoculars, a thermos and a backpack.

Frankie told the dealer she was planning to visit a friend in the area and asked if he could give her directions to the address. The dealer marked off the roads on one of Frankie's maps while she picked out some other equipment she needed. She stopped at a restaurant and picked up some take-out food, and spent the rest of the day in her motel room studying the map.

Alone in her room, Frankie Rose, the hardened, streetwise woman she had come to be, was lonely, and it hurt. She missed Ricardo. She had the overwhelming desire to call him. She knew he would be worried about her, but she also knew it was not the smart thing to do. *If I hang up quickly, they won't be able to find out where I'm calling from. Anyway, by the time he does find out, I'll be on my way home.*

Her heartache prevailed and she reached for the phone and asked the operator to dial her number. She lay still on the bed while the phone rang. A woman's voice answered.

"Maria," Frankie said excitedly. "This is Señorita Francine."

"Ay, Dios mio!" Maria screamed into the phone. "Oh, my God. The Señorita!" Frankie heard the phone drop. It was quiet for a few minutes. Then she heard a familiar voice.

"*Mi querida Francine* where are you? Why did you do such a foolish thing?" Ricardo asked.

"Ricardo, I miss you and love you."

"Then why did you run away?"

"Please listen to me. I don't have much time to talk. I am sorry I lied to you. But that bastard, Doc, had my brother killed. And now that I know where he is, I'm going to make him pay."

Ricardo yelled into the phone. "Damn it, Francine. Come home! It's too dangerous."

"Please Ricardo. I do love you, but I have to do this." Frankie hung up before he could say anymore. She thought the call would make her feel better, but it had the opposite effect. Hearing Ricardo's voice only made her miss him more. But this was important. Doc had to pay. She thought of Ricardo again, and tears came to her eyes. *Damn it, love really stinks.*

The next morning, Frankie stopped at a local deli to buy a hero and something to drink for her trip. She told the young man behind the counter that she was going to visit an old friend, and pulled out the directions the dealer from the camp store had given her.

"Do you know a shortcut here?" she asked him, pointing a finger to her destination on the map.

The young man scratched his head and told her there was another way to get there, but he didn't know if it was a shortcut. Frankie wrote down the information and left. She had decided to watch the place for a couple of days to see if Doc had any bodyguards hanging around.

Frankie followed the directions the clerk had given her, and found that the alternate road led her to a turnoff four miles before the main road to Doc's house. About eight miles farther along, she came to a man-made cutoff to the main road and pulled the car off the short road into some high dense foliage. It was about as secluded an area as she could find. She could sit on the hood of the car and watch the house through the clearing and still not be seen. She could also sneak over there at night if she wanted to.

Frankie settled down and waited and watched. Except for the mailman, who came about noon, no one else showed up. The late afternoon was a little busier. At one o'clock, while she ate her lunch, and between two and three o'clock, Doc had two visitors. Both looked like businessmen, and neither stayed long. She was curious about what he was up to, but knowing Doc, he probably had another con game going for himself.

She decided to wait one more day. There was no sense getting careless. She was about to leave, when she saw a car come off the main road, speeding towards the house. It skidded to a stop. Two men got out and rushed to the house. They were inside for fifteen minutes, and then both men came out, followed by Doc. She watched them on the porch, talking. One of them seemed to be pointing towards the wooded area around her. Then they left.

It couldn't be me they were talking about? I just got here, how could they know? She thought. *No, it's just a coincidence.* Frankie decided that maybe she should be more careful. Nobody but Doc knew what she looked like.

Except for the two clerks, she hadn't spoken to anyone that she could remember. *Well, I guess I'll go back to the motel and get something to eat and wait until tomorrow. It wouldn't hurt to wait one more day. Then all this will be over and I can rest easy.*

Frankie was up early the next morning. She was not feeling well. Perhaps she had caught a cold or something. She spent the morning looking for a doctor, explaining that she was new in town. Her stomach had been bothering her for a couple of weeks, she told the doctor, who wanted to run some tests. Frankie explained that she was going out of town on business in the morning and needed some medicine right away.

After a thorough examination, the doctor returned with the answer to Frankie's sickness. "Congratulations. You're pregnant! I'm going to give you something for the nausea until you can get home and see your own doctor."

* * * * *

Frankie was sleeping when the phone rang. It was her four o'clock wake-up call. She was feeling better, she decided, despite not having taken the medication the doctor prescribed. *After all of this, the pain I felt was just from being pregnant. Should I postpone this for tomorrow or should I just go home and let Ricardo handle it from here?* She asked herself. *No! I started this thing and I have to finish it. No! Since when did I ever need a man to finish what I started? Should I call Midge and tell her?* It was time to go and confront Doc. On the way, she stopped at the local gas station to fill up her thermos with coffee and two ready-made sandwiches. She figured she would get there just before dark. The weather had turned chilly, and she brought her jacket along. The forecast warned that the hurricane that had hit Georgia and the Carolinas, and was heading inland towards New York unless it changed directions, but it would strike inland by midnight.

Frankie had already made her decision. *There is nothing to do now but wait it out.* As darkness settled in, the lights in the house went on. She never realized how dark it got in the woods. It was scary --- like living in another world. Frankie watched the house, and sipped some coffee from the thermos. The wind had picked up a bit, and she pulled her jacket around her tighter.

As she munched on her sandwich, she looked around. The sound of the wind crashing against the bushes was disturbing. She shuddered and took another sip of her coffee, waiting for the lights in Doc's house to go out. Frankie began to wonder if this was a good idea after all. Maybe she should come back tomorrow.

The wind was loud and beginning to moan. Frankie didn't hear Lester come on her right. He shined a flashlight in her face, blinding her for a moment.

She put her hands up against the bright light.

"What's up, baby?" Lester said, and laughed as she reached for her handbag. Another voice screamed in the wind. "I wouldn't do that if I were you."

Frankie turned towards the second voice and raised her hands above her head.

"What are you doing out here, sweet stuff?" he asked, already aware.

"Nothing. My car broke down. I was just looking to see if anyone was around so I could make a call and get someone out here to get me," Frankie lied.

Lester started to laugh.

"What's so damned funny?" she asked

"Did you really think you could come here into our town and not be noticed?" Tommy challenged.

"I don't know what you're talking about; you must have me mixed up with someone else," Frankie answered.

"Look, sweet stuff. Your name is Frankie Rose and you came here to get Mr. Epstein. Now get off the car."

Frankie slid off the car and stood looking straight ahead.

The lights in the house went off. Lester pointed his flashlight towards the bungalow, switching the light on and off three times. She saw the house light go back on and off three times, then stay on. Lester grabbed Frankie by the shoulder and pushed her toward Tommy, who grabbed her by the wrist and spun her around. Lester took her backpack off the hood and searched it. All he found was a half eaten sandwich and half a thermos of coffee. Lester threw the backpack into the bushes.

"Tie her up," Tommy ordered.

As Lester passed Frankie, she stuck out her foot and tripped him. Before Tommy realized what was happening, Frankie had kicked Lester in the knee. He lost his balance completely and fell over. She swung around and smacked Tommy in the face with her bag, catching him off guard.

She turned to kick Lester again, but Tommy hit her in back of the neck with the butt of his forty-five. Frankie fell to the ground, unconscious. Lester got up and kicked her in the chest.

"See what else is in the car," Tommy said.

Lester took a quick look. "Nothing else except her shoulder bag."

"Give me a hand throwing her into my car."

"Mr. Epstein is going be real pleased that we got her."

"Yeah, he's going to get a laugh at the way you found her," Lester joked.

"So it was by accident that we found her. But if I hadn't gone into the deli to order a ham and cheese on rye, I would never have met the delivery boy."

Lester shrugged. "So what's the big deal? We got her didn't we?"

"I guess so. You take her in her car and I'll take mine and meet you at Epstein's."

"Let's go. The weather is getting really bad. I think the forecast said we were going to get a hurricane."

"Why don't we just kill her right here and save everyone a lot of trouble?" Lester suggested.

"No, Mr. Epstein said not to do anything until after he talks to her. Then we'll do whatever he pays us to do with her."

They drove both cars over to Doc's house. The wind had picked up, and the first drops of rain had started to fall. Then it cascaded like someone had opened the floodgates of heaven.

* * * * *

Doc opened the door as soon as the three of them reached it. Tommy pushed Frankie into the foyer.

"Easy, Tommy. That's no way to treat a good friend," Doc said with a sly smile.

"You wanted her, you got her. All she had with her was a pair of binoculars that she's been using to watch you and a backpack with some half eaten food. Her shoulder bag is still in the car," said Tommy.

"Bring her into the living room." Doc ordered.

Tommy dragged Frankie into the living room and pushed her onto the sofa. "What do you want us to do now?" Tommy asked.

"Go into the kitchen and have a drink. Get something to eat. I'll call you when I need you." Doc looked at Frankie and shook his head. "Why couldn't you just walk away like I asked you to? If you had, none of this would be necessary."

Frankie stuck out her chin. Her dark eyes were filled with hatred. "Why, you bastard! You had Jay killed. Then you tried to have me killed twice, all because of your greed, that's why."

"I realize I went about this in the wrong manner, so why don't I make amends? I'll give you your half of the loot and you go your way and I'll go mine," Doc said.

"You must really think I'm stupid."

"How can you say a thing like that?"

"Well, let me see… you killed four people, you tried to kill

180

me. You had me beat up twice. And now I'm tied up on your sofa. What do you think all that means?" Frankie asked sarcastically. "Oh, not to mention the fact that you sent Theo to get me. Fortunately for him, he saw the light."

"Frankie, you were always a smart ass. I wondered what happened to him. Well, I had enough of this little game."

"But I'm curious about one thing. How did you find me? Did you get the information from Theo?"

"No, Doc. Theo was loyal to you right to the very end, considering he knew you were going to kill him. And that's more then you deserve. It was one of your clowns in there --- they called you from my apartment, where they were waiting for me to show up. Midge had one of her cop friend's get a list of numbers and, bingo, your alias came up. If they hadn't have pulled the telephone out of the wall, I never would have known they had made a call."

"Good help is so hard to find these day." Doc said with a smile.

"Oh, and that phony relative you hired to mourn your passing. Good touch, but stupid" Frankie added.

"Sometimes a mistake can be a good thing; it got you here. Doc said with confidence. "I may have the boys in there look Midge up before I go... "

"Are they going to be around that long?"

"You really know how to hurt me, don't you?"

"No, Doc, but you must admit people who work for you don't seem to live long these days."

"You know I just wanted to discourage you. That's all I wanted."

Frankie laughed. "Doc, I'll say it again. You must think I'm stupid. Not only did you rob Ricardo Montoya of ninety million dollars in diamonds, not sixty like you said, but there were twenty five kilos of heroin you neglected to mention to anyone. How you managed to get the stuff out without your fellow thieves knowing it defies me, and that wasn't enough for you was it?"

"No Frankie I have a big appetite."

"Yeah, very big," Frankie mocked, pointing at his widening girth. "Ricardo Montoya is going to cut your head off."

"How do you know about Montoya?" Doc asked annoyed.

Frankie grinned. "Oh, wouldn't you like to know?"

Doc was annoyed and slapped her across the face. "I asked a question!"

Blood trickled down the side of her lip. She spit at him and Doc slapped her again, making her dizzy.

"You bastard. I'm going to kill you. You want to know how I know. He told me so!" Frankie yelled.

"I guess it doesn't matter anyway. You're history," Doc said nonchalantly.

"I'll see you in hell, you bastard!" Frankie yelled

"Maybe, maybe not. Because for now, it's too late for you. Your luck just ran out. My friends out there are going to see to it that you have a little accident."

"You can kill me, but Ricardo is going to find you, and when he does, he's going to cut your heart out."

"Ricardo, is it? I see we're on a first name basis. Still, I believe I have covered my tracks very well. And after you're gone and I disappear, no one will ever find me," Doc bragged.

"I found you and so will he."

"I always said you were smart, Frankie. But there is such a thing as being too smart. Well, you know what they say --- curiosity killed the cat. I would like to make one correction: you have run out of lives. He's going to find something, and it's going to be you. Dead, that is.

Doc called out to Tommy and Lester. "Get her out of here now. Take her to the quarry and kill her."

* * ⋈ * *

Driving to the quarry in two cars was much more dangerous in the teeming rain. Lester had run up on Tommy twice and had almost forced him off the road. The twenty-minute ride took more than an hour. Lester drove the rental car to the edge of the quarry and ran back to the boarded up office, where Tommy had Frankie already inside. He threw her shoulder bag on one of the lounge chairs.

Frankie managed to stand. "Are you going to untie me now?" she asked.

Lenny came in, dragging the wind and rain behind him. "What's up? Lenny asked.

"This smart ass wants me to untie her," Tommy replied.

"What does she think we are, stupid?" Lenny laughed. "I'm not going anywhere. Are you two tough guys afraid of me?" she taunted. "Shut up and sit down, or I'll whack you one," Tommy warned.

Frankie walked over to the lounge chair. Before she sat down, she pleaded, "Hey, at least tie my hands in front of me. How about it?"

"Lester, watch her and if she even looks like she is going to do anything, shoot her," Tommy untied her hands and retied them in front.

"Now sit down," he said, giving her a shove into the chair.

"Why don't we just kill her and put her in the car and then roll the car over the hill in the quarry now, not after the storm?" Lester suggested.

"No, Mr. Epstein wants it to look like an accident."

"For the first time in your life you may be right," Tommy said, walking over to the radio. "Let's see what's going on with the weather," he said, switching the radio on. The announcer was saying that there was a chance that hurricane Penny would blow out to sea, and that they would still get some gale force winds. They would know more in a few hours.

"Is there any more beer in the frig?" Lester asked.

"Yeah, there should be plenty. At least enough to wait out the storm," Tommy said.

"How about one for me Lester?" Frankie asked. Lester looked over at

Tommy for a sign.

"Go ahead, give her one."

Lester disappeared. Tommy sat at the desk sipping his beer and listening to the weather report. The lights flickered.

"Lester!" Tommy yelled.

"Yeah, what do you want now?" he asked grumpily as he entered the room buttoning his pants. "Where the hell do you think I was, damn it?"

"Keep an eye on her. I want to check the generator in case the lights go out," Tommy said, as he pulled on his raincoat and stepped outside into the storm.

Frankie stood up as Lester walked towards her. He tried to grab her, but Frankie pushed him away. Lester rushed her and pinned her to the wall. His weight was too much for her. As he lay against her, he pushed her legs wide apart, with one leg to keep her off balance. She couldn't move or kick him, so she shook her head from side to side violently to keep him from kissing her.

"Why are you fighting me, sweetheart? I want to put you in heaven before I kill you."

"Get off me, you bastard. I'd rather die first!" Frankie spit in his face.

Lester laughed. "Baby, it don't matter what you want, it's what I want that counts." Lester lay against her, using all his strength. He grabbed her face with both hands and bit her lip. Blood streamed down her chin. Lester laughed wildly, as

Frankie struggled to free herself. He stepped back to unzip his pants. Frankie brought the heel of her foot down on Lester's ankle with as much force as she could muster, and he fell back screaming with pain. "You bitch! You broke my ankle. I'll kill you for this!" Lester rolled on the floor screaming in agony as he grabbed his ankle with both hands. .

Frankie managed to get her hands free as he fell to his knees. She grabbed his face as he pulled out his gun and raked his face with her nails. Lester screamed and cried at the same time. She grabbed the gun from him and kicked him in the groin. Frankie backed up as he came towards her like a wild animal. She pulled the trigger and fired twice, hitting him in the chest. He reeled back before hitting the ground.

Tommy ran into the room and for an instant looking like a deer caught in the headlights. "Lester!" he yelled and ran to kneel by his brother. Frankie fired at him, the first two slugs ripping through the wood door.

Tommy drew his gun and fired three times at her. Frankie felt the searing pain rage through her as she backed up against the wall. Tommy came towards her. Darkness was setting in and her head was spinning. Frankie lifted her arm and pulled the trigger. Then everything went black.

* * * * *

Frankie awoke to the relentless slamming of the office door. She sat up, waiting for her eyes to focus. They were both dead. Lester lay a few feet from her and Tommy lay near the door. Frankie managed to stand and staggered to the bathroom. Frankie then leaned forward. Balancing herself against the sink, she put a hand towel soaked with water against the gash that the bullet had put in her side, and then threw up. Slowly making her way to the door, she felt queasy again. Frankie bent down and painfully went through Tommy's pockets for the car keys. The noise of the door opening and closing kept her jumping as the windswept rain sprayed the room each time the door opened.

Frankie managed to get her jacket on. Then, picking up her tote bag, she staggered outside. The wind had blown her rental off the edge of the gravel pit onto the rocks below. Frankie fell, lying in the mud, crawling to the car bumper, and holding on to it for support so she could stand; she then managed to get into the car. The pain was almost unbearable. She closed her eyes for a moment. *Am I ever going to see Ricardo again? I'm going to die here.*

PART THREE

CHAPTER TEN

MISSING PERSON

Midge was sunning herself by the pool when the maid came in announcing, "Miss Junco, there are two gentlemen at the door who say they are policemen, and want to see you."

"Tell them to come in, Ida, oh, and bring me another glass of ice tea," Midge said casually. The maid led the two men over to her. Midge looked up at them. "What can I do for you boys? If it's a donation you want I gave at the office," Midge joked.

"We would like to ask you some questions. About a Frankie Rose."

"Has anything happened to her? Is she all right?"

"I want to know where she is."

"Do you two have any identification? I don't believe you showed me any," Midge said trying to drag this conversation on.

Both men showed their identification. "I am Detective Mike Compton. And this is Detective Adam Ross. Now let's not play games; where is Frankie Rose?"

The maid came out with a pitcher of ice tea, and Midge waved then to the chairs. "Sit down, guys. Please have some ice tea. And I will answer any questions you have. But what is your interest in Frankie?"

Detective Compton removed his jacket. Wiping his face with his handkerchief, he roared, "Listen, I want to know where she is, and I want to know now!"

Midge jumped up. "Listen, you two boy scouts, get the hell out of here! And don't come back without a warrant."

188

"Wait," Detective Ross said. "You will have to excuse my partner. No one ever taught him manners. This is not an official visit."

"Then what are you doing here. And why are you so interested in her?" Midge asked.

"A friend asked me to do him a favor. I think you know who that friend is," Ross said. There was sign of relief in her voice. Montoya was still in New York. Midge told them the story that Frankie and she had rehearsed. They seemed to be convinced that she was telling the truth. Before they left, Detective Ross thanked Midge for her help, saying, "She called Mr. Montoya yesterday and he said she sounded as if she was sick." Then both men left.

A few minutes later, Karen walked out to the pool area. "Morning, sleepy head," Midge called out.

"Who were they?" Karen asked.

Midge explained who they were and that she had told them the rehearsed story. "I don't like the part about her not feeling well; that kind of bothers me," Karen said.

"I know she wasn't feeling good when she left me. I promised her I would not tell where she was; now I have to re-think this thing." Midge said, concerned.

"I really think you should." Karen replied.

"I will. Too bad you're leaving Wednesday. What do you say we do the town tonight?" Midge asked.

"Sounds good to me. I think I'll have a swim before breakfast," Karen said, as she jumped into the pool.

* * * * *

Karen was just finishing breakfast when Midge said, "You know, Karen, I shouldn't have let her go alone. Now that I think of it, she wasn't feeling good that whole week."

"What was wrong with her?" Karen asked.

"I didn't know she was sick every morning. You know... like she was nauseous." Karen started laughing.

"What's so funny? Midge asked.

"I thought you two were women of the world. Boy was I wrong. Especially about you, Midge."

"You going to tell me I'm not?"

"She is pregnant; at least that's what it sounds like." Karen said.

"My God how stupid I've been."

"You know you have no choice but to tell Ricardo about her," Karen said.

"No. I have to go there and get her before anything happens to her," Midge replied.

"Don't be stupid. Use your head. You'll never get to her in time to do anything. She has either done it by now, or is on her way to do it. Call Ricardo. He may be able to get to her first," Karen added.

"I don't know. I have already lied to him and he may not believe me. Suppose she isn't pregnant? I'm in deep shit anyway, so maybe there's a chance I could get there first," Midge said.

"Stop being so stubborn. As long as he gets to her before anything happens to her that's all that counts, besides, he has his own jet ready whenever he needs it."

"Midge, either you call him or I will; Frankie's pregnant. Now things have changed." Karen pleaded.

* * * * *

Antonio stood quietly as his boss, Ricardo Montoya, yelled at him. "How did you manage to lose one woman?"

Señor Montoya, I don't know... everything happened so

fast. The woman I followed looked like Señorita Frankie."

"Listen to me, think. Is there anything else you can remember to make it a little easier to find her?" Ricardo asked.

"Yes, there is, she looked like Señorita Frankie, but when I got up close to her. I thought she looked like someone I knew. But it couldn't be her. She is in Europe now. But she said not to worry, that she was sure that the Señorita was in good hands, then she winked at me and walked away," Antonio remembered. "I am beginning to understand now, the old bait and switch routine, I really should have known," Ricardo laughed sarcastically, and added, "You may go now, but stay close."

Ricardo called his secretary, Mrs. Rios, asking her to find out if Karen was still in the hospital. He also requested that she get in touch with Detective Compton in Miami, and have him call as soon as possible. He already had people checking on the number Frankie had used to call him. Ricardo was worried about her. She did not sound good to him. Maybe she was sick. *She said she would drive me crazy, now I know she meant it,* Ricardo thought. Whatever had to be done would have to wait until the hurricane warnings were over. They had been lucky this time. Except for the high winds they weren't affected very much.

Ricardo had his Lear jet on standby as soon as it was safe to take off. *Women,* he thought. *The three of them conspired to pull their scheme right under his nose.* There was nothing to do now but wait. Ricardo did not like the idea of not being in control. It seemed that his whole life had spun out of control when he met Frankie.

He answered the phone on the first ring. "Yes, this is Ricardo Montoya speaking. "Mr. Montoya, this is Detective Compton."

"Yes, I have been waiting for your call. What did you find

out?"

"I spoke to the Jingo woman. She gave me some story about Frankie going off somewhere to think things over. But I have to tell you. I think she is lying," the detective said.

"I believe you're right, Detective."

"You want me to lean on her a while?"

"No, I will handle the rest from here. Thank you."

"There is one thing... before I left, I saw a dark haired woman watching from a window, if that's any help." Before hanging up, the detective said that it could not have been Frankie, it had to be Karen.

The phone rang again. It was Ricardo's secretary. Mr. Montoya. I checked with the doctors as you requested. Karen Holms went on Holiday to Miami before the final series of operations began."

"Aha, just as I thought. Thank you, Mrs. Rios." Karen had to be in on the switch. He almost felt sorry for Antonio, because he never had a chance. They had out-smarted the both of them from the very beginning. The phone rang again and Ricardo answered it. "Hello, this is Ricardo Montoya speaking."

"Ricardo. This is Midge. Look, I have something to tell you, but first I am sorry I had to lie to you. But now there is something important I have to tell you, something I don't even think she knows."

"My God, woman if you know something say it!" Ricardo demanded.

"I know where Frankie is, and I am worried about her."

"Then why did you help her do this foolish thing?"

"I helped her out of friendship and loyalty, but what I didn't know then...was Frankie is pregnant." Midge could hear the heavy breathing on the other end.

"What are you saying, Señorita?"

"What part of pregnant didn't you understand?"

"A baby, she is going to have a baby? How do I know this is not part of your plan?" Ricardo said, disbelieving what he heard.

"You can believe it, my friend. Why do you think I'm calling you now?" Midge gave Ricardo Doc's new name and address, telling Ricardo to hurry before anything happened to Frankie. Ricardo's heartbeat quickened, as he knew that it was very lucky to get a second chance. He bowed his head and made the sign of the cross. "Heavenly father," he said, "I make no excuses of how I lived my life, but please don't take her from me. Let the woman I love and my baby live. And I will leave this life of crime behind me." Then, wiping his eyes, he yelled out, "Antonio, have the plane ready to leave within the hour."

"But the storm, Señor. The winds have not died down. Perhaps tomorrow."

Ricardo walked to Antonio and said, "Listen to me... Señorita Frankie is going to have my baby, so we must get to her before anything happens to her."

"Baby?" Antonio repeated then he ran out of the room. Ricardo had a renewed sense of purpose. He had grown up in poverty and was the youngest of seven children. His father was a laborer working for a rich farmer, while his mother took in washing. As the years passed, he had watched his older brothers struggle to succeed. The odds were against a person trying to get an education or even becoming wealthy. He loved his parents for how hard they had worked and went without many things to get his brothers and himself what little education they could.

Ricardo had made his decision at the age of twelve that he would become a member of the underworld. An educated thief would always succeed, and success would bring wealth. His illegal activities managed to keep him in school and obtain a college degree. It was his skill as a moneymaker that had allowed him to receive notoriety and it was then that Don Louise Diego noticed him, dubbing him king of thieves. It was Diego who had taken him under his wing to teach him all that he knew now.

Ricardo had invested in several legitimate businesses, knowing that someday he would decide to retire from this life.

Antonio came bursting through the doors. "Señor Montoya, the pilot said that he can't get clearance to take off. He said we should be able to leave by tomorrow."

"Tomorrow may be too late. I will fly the plane myself! Damn the weather." yelled Ricardo.

"But, Señor Montoya, this is a dangerous thing you do."

"If you are scared of the danger ahead, I will replace you with someone who is not!"

Antonio's face reddened. "Señor Montoya, many times I have put myself in peril, and so has Miguel, to keep you out of harm's way. You have never questioned my loyalty before, Señor; you know I would fight *el Diablo* himself to keep you from harm. But what good would it do for Señorita Frankie if anything happened in the plane?"

Ricardo was silent, frowning at Antonio, who had dared to speak to him in that manner, but he was right.

Antonio stepped back. Señor, please forgive my arrogance, I am ashamed, and if it was not for me we would not have this problem."

"No, Antonio, this is not your doing. We were both pawns in this deception. You are right about the plane; we will wait another four hours and no more. If we have to I will fly the plane myself." Ricardo hesitated then said, "Antonio, I do not question your valor or your honor. This has been a very bad day."

"Antonio, go get me some coffee and then get some rest. We have a difficult day ahead of us."

Ricardo Montoya thought back to the first time he met Frankie. She was a woman who could not be bought and paid for with money or jewels. If she had not come of her own free will, he would have had to let her go. He knew you could not tame a free spirit. He felt helpless sitting here. The woman he loved was going to have his child, and she was now in danger and there was nothing he could do about it. He laid his head back and closed his eyes, but sleep did not come easily. Ricardo was awakened by Antonio's knocking on the door. Ricardo stood up, calling out, "Come in, come in."

"Señor Montoya. The pilot called and we are cleared to leave whenever you are ready!" Antonio said, excited.

"That is good news. Get me Miguel quickly."

Antonio disappeared and was back in a few seconds with Miguel.

"Go quickly to Doctor Gilby and tell him to bring his black bag. There may be some wounds to heal, plus a pregnant woman. Be back within the hour."

Miguel rushed out of the room on his errand.

"Antonio, pack our gear; we may need it. Have the driver get the limo ready to go within the hour." Picking up the phone, he called the Embassy. "Jon, I have an emergency and am sending Miguel to get Doctor Gilby. Secure the helicopter and a crew of paramedics ready to travel within an hour's notice. Jon, I do not care where you get them, but get them, and no, I have no time to explain except to tell you my future wife's life is at stake." Ricardo hung up and prepared to leave.

* * * * *

Miguel arrived at the Doctor's office and told the driver to keep the engine running. Miguel ran into the building, up one flight of steps taking them two at a time, running down the hallway. The walls were lined with pictures covering the vine-covered wallpaper. Miguel ran into the waiting room. The nurse greeted him, "We're closed for the day, sir."

"I have come from Señor Montoya." Miguel explained briefly what Ricardo had told him.

* * * * *

It took Miguel twenty minuets to get to the private Airport. Ricardo was giving last minute instructions to his staff on his car phone as the limo skidded to a stop. Miguel exited the car and opened the back door and reached in, helping the doctor and his nurse out. Ricardo greeted the doctor as he started up the steps into the jet. "I am terribly sorry about this, but it is an extreme emergency. I will explain in more detail the moment we are in the air!" Ricardo said. Being an experienced pilot himself, Ricardo was in the co-pilot's seat as they took off.

* * * * *

The jet had leveled off, and Ricardo walked to the area where Doctor Gilby and his nurse were seated. He said, "Mr. Montoya, I realize that I am your physician, but I do resent the rough treatment by your bodyguard!"

"I am sorry to have offended both you and Nurse Benson, but this was an emergency." Ricardo then explained what had happened, leaving out certain facts. "And there was no time to organize anything," he continued. "This is a life and death matter. I will compensate both of you handsomely when this is over."

Both the doctor and nurse seemed to have calmed down, so

Ricardo walked to the lounge and sat down closing his eyes. *Nothing had been normal since he had met Frankie. She had turned a disciplined and mythical world into roller coaster ride. Is this the price of love?* He wondered. Considering the hurricane had just passed, there wasn't much turbulence. They should make Burlington in about two hours, so there was nothing to do but wait.

* * * * *

The jet taxied off the main runway and moved to a private hanger owned by an associate of Ricardo's. As the jet came to a stop and the passenger door opened, two cars pulled up. Ricardo and Antonio, along with the doctor and nurse, entered the green Dodge. Miguel met two other men and jumped into a red Buick, and then both cars sped away. As the car turned off the airport road onto the major highway, the driver handed Ricardo a folder with directions to Doc's house. Also, he was told that she could be at the quarry. He asked Ricardo what his orders were. They would go on to the farmhouse, where she would most likely be. The driver of Miguel's car was told to go to the quarry first and check it out. Ricardo wanted to cover all the bases. The car moved along at a steady pace. No one spoke, and Antonio could feel the tension in the air. "Señor Montoya. I have the feeling that the Señorita will be all right."

"I hope you are right, Antonio," Ricardo said dryly

Entering the road to the quarry, the car slowed down. They had expected to see a great deal of activity. What they found was deserted. Quarry trucks and equipment lay idle. The car stopped twenty yards from the office, and Miguel ordered the men to spread out. The three men approached the office building slowly. The door was half ripped off, the top hinges just barely holding on. Miguel had his gun out as he entered the office. Among the debris strewn about the room from the storm he found the two dead men. The other man came in. "Miguel, Jack is checking the outside."

The other man raced in to the office yelling, "There is a car wreck at the bottom of the pit."

Miguel ran out to the car, with the other two men following him. They sped down the winding truck route, almost going over the edge twice. The car reached the bottom and Miguel jumped out. He ran to the demolished car, and then breathed a sigh of relief to find the car empty. There was no evidence that anyone was in the car when it drove off the edge.

Above, one of the men was going through the dead men's pockets for their identification. Miguel called Ricardo from the car phone, "Senior Montoya, she is not here, but there are two dead bodies. The men seem to be related, and there is a wrecked car at the bottom of the quarry! He paused, listening for instructions, then said, "Yes, I will see to it."

Miguel had his orders to see that everything was cleaned up as if nothing had ever happened, then to meet them at the farmhouse. Miguel made several phone calls to the people who did the clean up. Miguel had noticed that there was a blood trail leading outside, indicating Frankie had been shot. This worried him. Not just for her sake, but for Ricardo's sake also. Quickly, he related what he had found to Ricardo.

* * * * *

As a young man, Miguel had found himself in trouble many times. He had always believed it was fate that brought him to Ricardo Montoya. Some one tried to assassinate Ricardo Montoya, and he happened to be in a good position. He grabbed the gunman, relieving him of his weapon, then broke the man's neck. Ricardo rewarded him by giving him a job. He was sent to the police academy for training. Ricardo had also taken care of his family; there was nothing he would not do for him. Now that his boss was retiring, the new patron would have his own men, and he would be out of a job. This did not make him happy, but perhaps there would be more time to spend with his wife, Amanda and his two sons. Miguel had hoped that his boys would follow the professional path, and not his. It would be nice to have a doctor in his home. But they were young and there was still time. They were lucky not to grow up as he did.

CHAPTER ELEVEN

NOBODY LIVES FOREVER

The driver skidded off the road onto the circular driveway. Slamming on the brakes, he maneuvered the car sideways, parallel to the sixty-foot oak tree that had been uprooted. Ricardo and Antonio jumped from the car, climbing over the oak tree with guns drawn, and then ran towards the house. Ricardo fell as he was going up the stairs. Antonio stopped to help him. "No, Antonio keep going," Ricardo yelled. Holding his Beretta up, he kicked the door in. As he entered the foyer, Ricardo was beside him now. The trail of blood led from the foyer to the living room. Both men were breathing heavily. Ricardo's pants were ripped, his knee was bleeding.

* * * * *

A banging noise woke Frankie. Rays of sunlight shone through the ripped window shade. Her head was spinning from the previous night. Frankie tried to clear the fog that was in her head; she was a bit dizzy, but she managed to hold on to the brass bedpost. The bed was covered with blood. Looking at her side, she saw that she was covered in dry blood; her stitches had torn open during the night. She heard the noise again and put on one of Doc's T-shirts that had been left on the bedpost. It was too big for her, but she didn't care. Frankie's head was a little clearer now, so she walked slowly to the bedroom door. She was weak from the loss of blood. With the .38 caliber in her left hand, her arm remained at her side as if she didn't have the strength to lift it. Walking slowly towards the stairs,

Frankie stood at the edge of the steps. Looking down, she saw him on the fourth step, holding on to the banister to keep his balance, his blood soaked shirt staining the railing. He had his gun tucked into his pants. Doc smiled, but it was a painful one. "Don't look so surprised, it's me, kid. As you can see, I am not that easy to kill." Doc coughed, spitting up blood.

Frankie held her gun, lifting the .38 and aiming it at Doc. Her head ached and streams of sweat clouded her vision. Her arms were shaky as fear shot through her. Frankie didn't know how long she could hold the gun up. She tightened her finger on the trigger. She pulled tighter, her strength waning as she tried to pull the trigger. Doc had an automatic in his hand. He pointed it at Frankie, trying to smile. He watched Frankie at the head of the stairs, her body shaking.

"You're finished, kid. After all this, you can't even pull the trigger. It don't matter anymore. I'm dying. And you're going right along with me."

"I told you I would meet you in hell," Frankie managed to say. Weakening, she fell against the railing post. Both guns went off at the same time, and Doc fell backwards, landing at the head of the stairs. The .38 dropped from her hand and toppled down the stairs.

* * * * *

The yellow gold enhanced the beauty of the white silvery clouds. Frankie felt no pain as she floated in the arms of the waiting mist and was held gently and out of harm's way. All the tension and the hurt were gone. Floating through the heavens, she not knowing destination, but feeling the awe of being held firmly. Frankie could hear the faint voices in the mist. The voice was gently calling her name quietly. She tried to answer. But no words came out of her. Frankie curled her body up. Waiting, for what she did not know.

CHAPTER TWELVE

LIFE OR DEATH

Ricardo sat at the edge of the steps cradling Frankie in his arms. "Please, God don't take her from me!" he said, holding back the tears. He felt someone pulling at him. It was Doctor Gilby and his nurse.

"Get the hell out of the way. And let me do the job you brought me to do!" snapped Doctor Gilby. "Nurse give me my bag."

Ricardo laid her down gently, taking off his jacket and rolling it up to make a pillow for Frankie's head.

"How is she, Doctor?" Ricardo asked.

"Not good. You," he pointed at Antonio. "Get her to bed then get him out of here! I need room to work."

They put her in bed, then Antonio gently grabbed Ricardo by the arm.

"Señor Montoya, please come downstairs with me. There is nothing we can do now. She is in God's hands."

"But I must be with *mi querdo,* Francine."

"No, Señor, you must come with me downstairs.

"Yes, I suppose you're right, Antonio."

Both men walked down the stairs. As Miguel ran in and started to ask questions, Antonio motioned for him to be quiet. Then Antonio walked with Ricardo to the porch and sat him down. Walking inside the house with Miguel he said, "*Amigo,* things do not look good for the Señorita." His tone was grave

"What will we do?" Miguel asked.

Then they heard the doctor yell out, "One of you come up here, quick!"

Both men ran up the stairs quickly.

"What is it?" Miguel asked.

"I want you to listen to me. I sewed up her stitches and I have done everything I can do. She has lost a lot of blood. I have some plasma, but not enough unless she gets to a hospital for a transfusion as quickly as possible. She is going to die without it."

"It has already been taken care of; a helicopter is on the way," Miguel said.

"If I knew her blood type, it would help. Even if I did though, I would still need a blood donor." Antonio picked up the shoulder bag and dumped the contents on the floor. He rummaged through the items and picked up a letter from Doctor Clark. Opening it, he read the contents. The papers explained the tests that had been preformed on her. Reading the results, he yelled out to Miguel who came over to him, "Read this. Doctor, she is Type O."

"Her life is at stake and, according to this paper your friend here gave me, so is her baby."

"I have Type O blood," yelled out Miguel.

"And I am Type O, also, Doctor," Antonio said.

"Nurse, prep both of them."

Antonio took the papers and quickly ran down the stairs to the porch, while Miguel gave the first pint of blood. As Antonio ran down, he met his boss.

Antonio handed him the papers, but Ricardo still could not believe what he was reading.

"Señor Montoya, if Señorita Frankie is to live, she is in need of blood. Both Miguel and I have Señorita's type blood. When Miguel is finished, I will give mine, and by then, the helicopter will be here," Antonio said.

"I hope you are right," Ricardo said in a depressed tone.

"The little fool, knowing she was going to have a child and

to do this. Antonio what am I to do with her?" Antonio
managed to smile. "As you always say Señor, the Señorita is
incorrigible.

* * * * *

Ricardo looked subdued. He had always been a man of
action. He had always been able to make snap decisions. *Pull
yourself together, Ricardo,* his inner voice ordered. Ricardo
stood up. *I must look in on* mi querdo Frankie. Ricardo walked
up the stairs slowly this time. He entered the bedroom. The old
blood stained sheets were piled in the corner of the room.
Antonio had just finished giving blood.

"How is she?" he asked the nurse.

"She must have a great deal of inner courage. Her body is
fighting to live. And that's half the battle. I know I shouldn't
say this, but without the extra blood, no matter how strong she
is, she would never have made it through this ordeal," Nurse
Benson said.

"Do not worry. She will live. You will have all the blood
you need within the hour."

"You are a most amazing man," Nurse Benson said in awe.

"I will like to sit with her for a while. Why don't you go
downstairs and take a break."

Nurse Benson smiled and nodded, then she left.

Ricardo sat down by Frankie, and for the first time in his
life he had the feeling of helplessness. All he could do was
hold her hand and talk to her, not knowing if she could hear
him or not. She was restless, and talking to herself,
incoherently. Ricardo checked his watch. Ten minuets seemed
like an hour. *Where the hell are they?*

Antonio came in standing by his side. "Señor
Montoya...how is the Señorita? I like her very much... She

once said I was silly," Antonio said smiling.

"And why was that?" Ricardo responded.

"Well, Señor," he said, "she said if I could I take her to lunch, why could I not eat with her, and why do I call her Señorita and Frankie instead of Francine? I tried to explain that I could never address her as just Francine. When I told her that it was a matter of respect to her and to you, she said it was a silly custom," Antonio said, amused.

"Antonio, do you think she will live?" Ricardo asked.

"Yes I do, Señor, she is a very strong-willed woman. And, she will live to bear you many strong and healthy children. If I myself am fortunate enough to find a woman of Señorita's caliber, I will be a lucky man," Antonio said without hesitation.

Ricardo stood up with pride. "Thank you Antonio. I have an important job for you when *mi querdo Francine* gets well. You will continue to be her personal bodyguard."

"If that is what you wish, I will do it," Antonio said.

* * * * *

The noise and vibration from the helicopter shook the old farmhouse as Miguel came running in. "Señor, they are here." Before Ricardo could reply, men with medical equipment flooded the room. Doctor Gilby ordered, "Okay, gentlemen, get out and stay out as we have a lot to do," and insisted that the door be shut.

As Miguel stepped outside, he said, "Señor, I took the liberty of sending the driver out for some food. And I have made some coffee for you."

"I could use some, thank you, Miguel."

"You will not thank him when you taste it," Antonio said, laughing.

"Señor, I have been looking around," said Miguel. "This Doc was indeed a very smart man. I opened the box with the bust of Cesar in it that had been molded with the heroin and it is all in one piece. If we ourselves had not done this many times, I would never have known." And then he produced a large damp cloth bag with the diamonds in it. "These were in the fish tank."

"That was excellent work, Miguel. Where is the body?'

"It's in the closet wrapped in a body bag. Our friends will drop it into the ocean on their way home."

"Tell them I am most grateful for their help. I will call our people to pick up our property.

"Are you sure, Señor Montoya?"

"Yes, I am, we will be too busy with other business matters."

* * * * *

Ricardo waited as the day turned to night. "What could be taking so long? All they had to do is sew up some stitches. Antonio, get me the doctor."

As Antonio stood to leave, the doctor approached them. "No need, I am here. We had some complications, but she is all right now."

Ricardo felt a heavy weight lifting and he sighed, "And the child?"

"Everything is fine. If it weren't for the blood these men gave, things would have been different," the doctor replied.

"Can I see her now, Doctor?" asked Ricardo.

"No, it's best she gets some rest. She has been through a great ordeal. The paramedics are ready to leave," the doctor said.

Ricardo walked out to the foyer to thank the men

personally. "Ah, Captain Forsite. It seams that every time I see you and your men, it's always an emergency. I want to thank all of you for your help," Ricardo said, shaking hands with each one of them.

"Let's just say it's all in the line of business, and everything will be fine," the Captain said.

Miguel felt that when his boss retired he would not be asked to stay on. He was not like Antonio. Too much pride prevented him from asking his boss to keep him as his bodyguard. One of the many legitimate businesses Ricardo owned was a private ambulance service. Miguel had called them and they would be waiting for them to arrive. Both men had decided to let their boss sleep a little longer. The driver and his assistant waited on the front porch for the order to get ready.

* * * * *

Miguel was sitting at the table having a cup of coffee when Antonio came in. Pouring some coffee, he sat down. "I will be glad when we are on our way home," Antonio said, yawning.

"I think you should get used to this country living when the Señor retires. He may choose to live in surroundings like this," Miguel said.

"Well, dear friend, so will you."

"I do not know if I will be staying."

Ricardo walked into the kitchen as Miguel spoke, interrupting him, "Ricardo said where would you be going?"

Miguel was silent.

"Speak up, I said."

"I am sorry Señor, I …"

Antonio broke in. "He thinks you will no longer need his services when you retire."

Ricardo laughed. "Both you and Antonio have been at my side for over twenty years. I have entrusted you both with my life and have been rewarded many times. If you want to go, I will not hold you, but I have no reason to let you go. Both of you are like my family to me, and does a man strip himself bare of his family? The answer is no." Ricardo added, "And as you both can see, taking care of my future wife is a full time job.

Ricardo shouted, "Get everyone ready! We will be leaving soon." Then he turned to leave the kitchen.

* * * * *

He was at her side now, and he sat on the side of the bed holding her hand. *"Mi querido, !e amao mucho."*

"Ricardo is that you?" Frankie asked in a singsong voice barely above a whisper.

Frankie had been in the hospital for two weeks. She smiled as Ricardo entered the room. "Ricardo, I want to come home, I miss you so much," she said, pouting.

"Yes, *mi querido*. It is time for you to leave here. I, too, miss you, and I have come to take you home," Ricardo said softly.

"Do you still love me after what I did, Ricardo?" she asked.

"I am angry at you for disobeying me, but *mi querido*, the answer is yes, I love you madly."

"Then, marry me now, today. We can have a church wedding later," she said excitedly.

"Yes, I will do that if it is your wish. But you must promise me one thing," Ricardo said softly.

"Anything Ricardo, ask me anything," Frankie said cheerfully.

"No more wild escapades."

"I promise," Frankie said.

"I wish Midge and Karen were here now," Frankie said sadly.

"But they are, they are waiting outside to see you."

Midge came in, followed by Karen. Midge hugged her. "I'm so happy you're okay," she said joyfully.

Karen kissed Frankie on the cheek. "You're crazy, but I love you. I'm glad you're safe.

"Ricardo, my bridesmaids are here. Let's get married."

* * * * *

Midge stood on the right side of the bed and Karen on the left. Antonio and Miguel stood at the side. The ceremony was small, but tearful, both women crying, and the ring was Ricardo's pinky ring. This was not the type of wedding he had planned, but if it made Frankie happy, it would do for now. When Frankie was well enough, they would go to Spain and have the big wedding that he had planned.

"Ricardo," she said, "Frankie Rose is retired, and Francine Montoya is born." Ricardo bent over and kissed her.

"Ricardo, can we go home now?" she said.

Bending over, he picked her up and cradled her in his arms as he gently placed her in a wheelchair.

Frankie dug her head into his shoulder, knowing no one could hurt her now. "Ricardo, are you sure you don't hate me for what I did?" She repeated, sounding unsure of herself.

"No, I told you I do not."

"Just checking," she said, sounding tired.

"Ricardo, I forgot to tell you, we're having a baby," Frankie said.

"Yes, I know *querida,* but you must be quiet and rest," Ricardo said as Antonio opened the door. The ambulance was waiting outside when they left the building.

"Ricardo," she said again.

"Mi querida, you must be quiet and rest," Ricardo begged.

"Ricardo, one more thing, please."

"What is it, *Cara*?"

"Ricardo, how high does our jet fly?"

"Twenty-five thousand, maybe thirty thousand feet, I believe. Why do you ask?" Ricardo questioned.

"Ricardo, did you ever have sex at thirty thousand feet?"

"Frankie, you are incorrigible."

Frankie snuggled closer to him. "I know, Ricardo."

Then she closed her eyes and fell into a peaceful sleep.

EPILOGUE

The Rolling Hills Girl's Academy lay deep in the sprawling mountains of North Carolina. Ricardo had some reservations about putting their ten-year-old daughter into a private school, but he had thought that Frankie was right about the child not only getting a better education, but that the discipline would be good for her. Both parents had blamed each other for spoiling their child, Angelica, who had the distinction of being the only youngster ever to be expelled from kindergarten.

They both sat in the outer office waiting for the Dean to see them. They had an eleven-fifteen appointment, and Frankie was the first to speak, "Ricardo, I wonder what she has done now?"

He turned to Frankie and said, "*Mi querdo* Francine. Knowing our Angelica, it could be anything."

"Ricardo, do you think there is a chance that someone switched babies on us at the hospital?"

Ricardo shook his head. 'No, I am sure that was not possible. Perhaps what is wrong is that she has too much of her mother in her."

"Oh, sure, blame me. But, I think *you* baby her too much."

"You realize that she has been expelled from two schools already, and she is only ten years old?"

They heard footsteps and Ricardo nudged Frankie. They both watched as they heard someone coming down the hall and they assumed it was Angelica's physical education teacher. Ricardo couldn't help but notice how much like her mother Angelica looked. And, like her mother, Angelica had that mischievous smile on her face.

When they reached the office, she greeted her parents,

"Hello, Mother, hello Father," Angelica said in a professional manner.

"I am going to *hello mother you* when I get you home," Frankie said. The door opened and they were asked to step inside by the woman who had escorted their daughter to the office.

Dean Stanton greeted them as they entered. Abigail Stanton was a short heavyset woman with a very stern look about her. "Mr. and Mrs. Montoya, I wish I could say this was going to be a pleasant meeting, but... well, this is Ender Mitchell, our physical education teacher. Going over my files, I find that Angelica has been expelled from two schools already. And the shame of it all is that she is a straight A student."

"You knew that when we entered her into your school last year," Frankie said.

"Yes, you are right, and there are some things that can be overlooked, but this is not one of those incidents."

Ricardo just sat there saying nothing.

"Well, what did she do this time that was so bad?" Frankie asked.

"What she did Mrs. Montoya...she managed to handcuff Miss Mitchell to a pole."

Ricardo stood up and looked over at his daughter. She smiled at him in her usual mischievous way. "Dean Stanton. I do not mean to dispute you, but how does a ten-year-old child not only get hold of a set of handcuffs, but how does she manage to handcuff a grown woman to a pole?"

"Miss Mitchell, would you tell Mr. Montoya what happened."

Ender Mitchell stood up. She was in her forties and very athletic looking. Her right arm was in a sling. "Angel, as we call her, said that she was doing a project for social studies and asked if I would help, and that her teacher had given her a note saying it would all right to be late for her class. She had her three cohorts show me the notes. By the way, the notes were forged. Then, she and her cohorts went about opening the water valves to both the indoor and outdoor pools, draining them, and if that wasn't bad enough, she found a weather balloon, God knows where she got it." Miss Mitchell sighed, then continued, "She picked the lock to the roof door, pulled the emergency water hose out and filled the balloon, and the three of them managed to roll it off the roof, almost killing the janitor when it fell."

"You keep saying her, but there were three of them," Ricardo said.

"You are right, Mr. Montoya, but she is the ringleader," the Dean said with authority.

"Is she sure one of these kids isn't named Midge?" Frankie muttered to herself.

"I didn't hear what you said," The Dean asked

"No matter," Frankie said, embarrassed.

The Dean added, "I overlooked the class where she taught her cohorts how to hotwire a car."

Frankie stood up, yelling at Angelica, "Where do you learn these things?"

Angel shrugged her shoulders and looked up at the ceiling.

"Angelica, I asked you a question, now answer me."

"I read a lot, Momma," Angelica said sweetly.

Ricardo said, "This is most embarrassing, and of course, I will compensate you for all damages the school has incurred. And, Miss Mitchell, I will pay any medical expenses you may incur. I would also like to donate two hundred thousand dollars to expand any facility you wish."

"So, can you recommend a good school?" Frankie asked the Dean.

"I have decided not to expel your daughter. But, for now, she is on two week's suspension."

* * * * *

They were standing in the parking lot where Frankie asked Antonio, "Did you teach her how to hotwire a car?"

"Señorita Francine, the young lady asks so many questions. I may have mentioned *it*."

"I thought so," Frankie said, turning to face Angelica. "Young lady, you are lucky you didn't kill yourself on that roof. You're grounded for six months. No, make that twenty years."

"Papa, will you teach me to drive?" Angelica asked sweetly.

"You're only ten years old, Angel. The answer is no."

"How about when I am fifteen, Papa?"

"I said no, you're too young. And besides, you're very irresponsible," Ricardo said.

"Papa, how about if I am responsible?"

"No," Ricardo broke in. "Angel, you are incorrigible. Do you know that?"

"You mean like Momma?"